"I've been looking forward to tonight all afternoon long."

"First you want me to pack and return to Chicago and then you tell me you've been wanting to go out with me. That's contradictory," Destiny said, but Wyatt saw the desire in her gaze.

"My feelings are contradictory," he said. "You're a complication in my quiet life." Her wide green eyes made him yearn to tell her to do whatever she wanted in Verity.

"A few complications in life sometimes makes it more interesting. You'll be able to handle this one, I'm sure."

"I can't wait to handle this complication," he said in a husky voice, his heart drumming as he looked at her full lips.

He knew she wasn't going to leave quietly. She would be a constant challenge to him...the most enticing challenge he'd ever had in his life.

* * *

A Texan in Her Bed is part of the Lone Star Legends series from *USA TODAY* bestselling author Sara Orwig

* * *

If you're on Twitter,
tell us what you think of Harlequin Desire!
#harlequindesire

Dear Reader,

What happens when a tall, laid-back Texas rancher wants peace and quiet and a stunning, feisty redhead barges into his life? West Texas billionaire rancher Wyatt Milan agreed, in a good deed for his town, to be sheriff. Now, just when tranquility is settling into his life and surroundings, Destiny Jones arrives to stir up old family feuds and bring national attention to the small Texas town. It was never part of Wyatt's job description that he would have to deal with a whirlwind redhead, but he's not a man to give up easily.

This is the second story of Texas families whose lives are changed by a legend passed down through the years. Our history influences our present. I grew up in a family with a long history of Texas and Tennessee legends and those legends still spark the imagination. They were a source for this story. Thank you for your interest in this book.

Sara Orwig

A TEXAN IN HER BED

—

SARA ORWIG

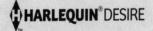
HARLEQUIN® DESIRE

Recycling programs
for this product may
not exist in your area.

ISBN-13: 978-0-373-73336-1

A TEXAN IN HER BED

This edition published by arrangement with Harlequin Books S.A.

For questions and comments about the quality of this book, please contact us at CustomerService@Harlequin.com.

® and TM are trademarks of Harlequin Enterprises Limited or its corporate affiliates. Trademarks indicated with ® are registered in the United States Patent and Trademark Office, the Canadian Intellectual Property Office and in other countries.

Printed in U.S.A.

™ www.Harlequin.com

Books by Sara Orwig

Harlequin Desire

Silhouette Desire

¤Stallion Pass
*Stallion Pass: Texas Knights
ΩThe Wealthy Ransomes
+Platinum Grooms
§Stetsons & CEOs
^Lone Star Legacy
‡Lone Star Legends

Other titles by this author
available in ebook format.

SARA ORWIG

lives in Oklahoma. She has a patient husband who will take her on research trips anywhere, from big cities to old forts. She is an avid collector of Western history books. With a master's degree in English, Sara has written historical romance, mainstream fiction and contemporary romance. Books are beloved treasures that take Sara to magical worlds, and she loves both reading and writing them.

With many thanks to Stacy Boyd, Senior Editor.

One

What Sheriff Wyatt Milan liked most about his job was that he knew what to expect in his quiet town of Verity, Texas. But on this October afternoon when he turned his car around the corner onto Main Street he knew change was in the air.

A red limousine took up his parking space, plus some, right in front of city hall.

"What the hell?" he said quietly.

"Gosh almighty, there goes a quiet afternoon," Deputy Lambert whispered. "Will you look at that," he said louder.

Wyatt was looking. Directly in front of the small city hall building stood a prominent sign with large letters: No Parking—Reserved for the Sheriff of Verity, Texas.

He had expected the usual big empty space where he could park Verity's official black-and-red sheriff's car. Instead, the red stretch limousine took every inch of the allotted area.

He and his family had money, as did many families in

the town, but no one owned anything as flashy as an all-red limo. "That limo doesn't belong to anyone living in these parts," Wyatt said, more to himself than to his deputy, thinking something was about to shatter some of the peacefulness of his hometown.

"In my whole life, I've never seen a limo that big and that red," Val said with awe in his voice. "I'll go look for the driver."

"He may be inside."

"No one was scheduled to see you today, were they?"

"No," Wyatt said, halting beside the limo. "You write a ticket and stick it on the windshield. Come in when you're through. If the owner or the driver isn't here, we'll go look around town for him. The people who live here want a quiet, peaceful town. I want one, too. Thanks to my sister marrying a Calhoun, the old Milan-Calhoun feud has finally died down. I don't want something happening to bring trouble elsewhere in town."

"Amen to that. Why would anyone park a big limo in the sheriff's space?"

"Either he's lazy, starting trouble, unobservant or he's someone who thinks he can do whatever he wants. Who knows?"

Deputy Lambert stepped out and Wyatt drove around the corner and parked in the alley behind the building, in the small space allotted for two cars and a nearby Dumpster. His life had had enough upheavals—an emotional breakup years earlier with his fiancée and then coming home to his brother fighting with a Calhoun neighbor, keeping the century-old family feud explosive. When people wanted him to run for sheriff of Verity County, based in the town of Verity, he'd had to quiet fights between his brother Tony and Tony's neighbor Lindsay Calhoun. Everything was finally coming under control. He didn't want someone to come to town and destroy the peace he had worked hard to establish. He shook his head as he entered city hall. He hoped this was settled quickly and quietly and the red limo drove out of Verity the same way it'd come in.

Entering the Verity County sheriff's office through the back door, Wyatt walked down the long hall. His boot heels scraped the scuffed boards as he passed the large file room, a small break room and a meeting room with a small table and chairs. The hallway continued, dissecting the stone building. To the right were the mayor's office, the town records office and the utilities office. To the left were the sheriff's office and a two-cell jail. The center reception area was lined with vinyl-covered benches and in the middle was a desk where a clerk sat. Wyatt looked at Corporal Dwight Quinby whose wide eyes sent a silent message that something was up here at the office. Dwight's tangled light brown hair became more snarled as he ran his fingers through it.

"Sheriff, there's a woman in your office. When she said she wanted to see you, I told her to have a seat out here, that you'd be back soon, but she talked me into telling where your office is and letting her go back there. I don't even know how she did it. First thing I knew she smiled and was gone," he said, sounding dazed.

"Dwight, slow down," Wyatt drawled quietly. "Who is she? What's her name?"

"I didn't get her name. I don't know—one moment she was here and the next she was in your office. I don't know what happened."

"Tell Val when he comes in that I've found the limo passenger. Tell him to look around town for a uniformed driver and get that thing moved out of my parking place. Or call Argus and tell him to come tow that limo away from here."

"You might change your mind after you meet her," Dwight said.

Startled, Wyatt shook his head. "I don't think so. You call and get it towed," he said, curious now who was waiting in his office and why Dwight would say such a thing or look so dazed.

"Yes, sir," Dwight replied, glancing through the oval glass in the front door that offered a good view of the red limousine.

"Sheriff, you haven't ever met anyone like her," Dwight said, surprising Wyatt even more with such an uncustomary reaction.

With a long sigh, Wyatt headed for his office. Whatever the woman wanted, she'd have to move the limo before they did anything else. He hoped she wasn't moving to Verity. The town was filled with enough affluent people who thought they had special rights and privileges. It took tact and diplomacy to deal with them, including his own family sometimes.

In this case, he felt the owner of the limo lost all rights to tact and diplomacy when she had the limo parked in the sheriff's space.

Wyatt opened the door of his office and walked in. Instantly he forgot all about the limo.

His gaze focused on a long-legged redhead seated in a leather wingback chair that was turned slightly toward the door. Big green eyes immobilized him, a sensation that Wyatt was unaccustomed to. With an effort his gaze left hers, trailing over her while his breath left his body. Dimly, he wondered if another movie was going to be filmed in or near Verity and this was the star. A riot of curly auburn hair spilled over her shoulders, giving her a sensual, earthy look that heated his insides. Flawless, smooth skin heightened her allure. Her green dress emphasized the color of her eyes and clung to a figure that threatened to melt his thought processes. Lush curves turned the room temperature to the heat of a West Texas summer. He noted her tiny waist, but then his gaze traveled down where the dress ended at her crossed knees, down long shapely legs.

"Well, good morning to the illustrious sheriff of Verity County," she said, drawing out her words in a throaty voice that sounded like a suggestive invitation to sin instead of a greeting.

Without conscious thought of what he was doing, Wyatt walked toward her. He stopped in front of her. A faint hint of a smile gave a slight curve to her full, red lips and he couldn't keep from wondering what it would be like to kiss her.

"Good morning. It's Wyatt Milan," he said, waiting for her to respond and give him her name.

She smiled and his knees almost buckled. Her smile was dazzling and lit up her face as if she were the friendliest person in the state of Texas, and in that moment he understood why his clerk had been so dazzled.

When she held out her hand, he took it, his fingers closing around a dainty, warm hand that sent electricity streaking through him. A beautiful pearl-and-diamond band was on one of her fingers. He glanced at her other hand to see it was bare of rings.

"I'm Destiny Jones, Sheriff Milan. I'm from Chicago."

As if she had plunged a knife into his heart, Wyatt came out of his daze. He had never met the woman, but he knew the name and he knew about her. His wits began to work again and his breathing steadied, and he could almost view her without an intense physical reaction. As if his emotions were on a pendulum, his feelings about her swung in the opposite direction and he viewed her as pure trouble.

"Destiny Jones, as in Desirée Jones's sister," he said, recalling the headline-making, temperamental, stunningly beautiful movie star he had once had an affair with while she was on location in Verity. An affair that had ended badly. He remembered Desirée talking about her older sister who hosted a television show about unsolved mysteries and had written a bestselling book, *Unsolved Mysteries of the South.*

"Ah, you remember," she replied.

"I always remember a beautiful woman," he said, his gaze traveling leisurely over Destiny's features even as his guard came up. Both sisters were breathtaking, but they were both probably casual about their relationships. He had known that with Desirée and he guessed that now about Destiny.

"I've been waiting three years to meet the illustrious sheriff of Verity, Texas, and now I finally get to do so," she said with a smile that threatened to melt the polar ice caps. "You're a Milan, the family involved in a feud with the Calhouns."

"So you know about the feud," he said, suspecting trouble was coming his way within hours.

He turned a leather chair to face her and sat only a couple of feet away. "So you're in town for what purpose?" he asked bluntly, mildly amused that she had taken his parking place, made herself comfortable in his office and now with him. He saw no reason to waste time in polite chit-chat. He was still idly curious, however, and he couldn't deny the thought of asking her to dinner crossed his mind.

"For one thing, I hope I can have an interview with you about the Lavita Wrenville house. I think it will be a wonderful subject for my *Unsolved Mysteries* television show."

Her words made him focus more rationally on her. He smiled only to be polite. The Wrenville house was where a Milan and a Calhoun had once fought over the same woman and both men, along with her father, had been shot to death. Century-old murders that could stir up the feud again.

"The Wrenville house," he said. "That place really isn't very interesting and there is nothing you can do at this time to solve the murders that happened in the house. That was over a century ago, old news with cold clues. At best, you might come back next year when the town of Verity has full rights to the property."

"That's interesting. I'd like to hear more about the town getting full rights. Even if I can't get a solution, I'd like to present the story about the house and family because it's unknown, unusual and I think it could be of interest to my audience."

"You might check Texas history because I think you'll find other unsolved mysteries that are far more fascinating in places far more appealing."

"That's interesting to know, too, Sheriff Milan," she said, giving him a sweet smile. "But I really want to do this one. And you should know I pursue what I want."

"And I imagine you're accustomed to getting what you want," he said, his gaze flicking over her. He guessed most men found it difficult to tell her no, especially with her devastating smile.

"That happens often," she said, leaning forward and shortening the gap between them. "I'm curious, Sheriff Milan," she said in a pleasant tone that probably ended most men's resistance, "why are you so set on discouraging me about the Wrenville house?"

"Verity is a quiet town with residents who like the status quo. As sheriff, I definitely like peace and quiet. If you'll look around, you won't find any tourist attractions. We do have a tiny museum, but it's not very interesting. Ditto our small library."

She smiled. "I assure you, I'm not planning to make this a tourist attraction. Maybe it's well you don't work for the Chamber of Commerce or the Tourist Center."

"We don't have a Tourist Center," he said quietly. "That should give you an idea."

From the moment he had discovered the red limo, this

woman had been surprising him, but her purpose for being here was an even bigger surprise—and an unpleasant one.

"I'm sorry you came all this way, Ms. Jones. You should have contacted me and I could have saved you the trouble. Lavita Wrenville was the last surviving Wrenville and she deeded the place to the town of Verity. According to the deed, we can't do anything to the grounds or house until next year, when it reverts totally to the town. I'm sheriff and I'm not opening that house."

"I am so sorry that you're unhappy about this, Sheriff Milan." Leaning back, she rummaged through a large purse. Gold bangles jingled on her arm and while her attention was on her purse, he looked her over from head to toe once again, his insides tightening as he envisioned her without the dress. As he gazed at her, she withdrew two envelopes and held them out to him. With a sinking feeling, he recognized the logo on one. "I wrote the governor of Texas, and I've written the mayor of Verity. I have letters from both stating clearly that I may look through the Wrenville house. Actually, I'm here as a guest of the state of Texas. You have such a nice governor. If you'd like to read the letters, here they are."

Wyatt held back a groan and resisted swearing. The last thing he wanted was someone stirring up the old family feud and drawing tourists who would want to walk through the Wrenville house. The dread that he experienced earlier—that his peaceful life and the public serenity of Verity were on the brink of destruction by one headstrong, sexy redhead—was coming true before his eyes.

A few moments later, after he'd read the letters, Wyatt made a mental note to talk to the mayor. Gyp Nash hadn't let him know one thing about Destiny Jones coming to Verity to see the Wrenville house. Gyp didn't like conflict, so that's probably why he had avoided telling Wyatt. But for the mayor to say how "thrilled" the townspeople would be that the Wrenville story would be the subject of one of her shows… Did Nash know this town at all?

He gave her back her letters. "Very nice," he said in clipped tones, trying to think what he could do to get rid of her.

"The Wrenville house is a big, dusty, empty house. There are all sorts of rumors and a legend about the property. People and kids have looked through it over the years until finally there's no interest in it. I want to keep it that way," he said. He felt a clash of wills with the charming, breathtaking bit of trouble that was sitting only a few feet from him. Along with the friction was a strong physical appeal that he didn't want, but couldn't shake.

"I suspect you've been through the house?"

"Oh, sure, when I was in high school. Kids used to be curious and there were all sorts of wild rumors, but they all died out. Ask people who have high school kids—there's no interest now. Jump back to my grandparents' generation and fights would break out over whether a Milan or a Calhoun shot first and killed the other as well as Lavita Wrenville's father that fatal night. In the three years that I've been sheriff we haven't had a fight break out over who fired the killing shots, nor have I had a trespassing call at the Wrenville place. It'll be better for the Calhouns and the Milans when the old house is gone. It serves as a reminder of the feud."

"Well, I'm curious and you're not discouraging me. It's a fascinating story of three unsolved murders and perhaps a hidden fortune. That's an intriguing mystery."

"Not really. There were three murders, but they took place in the late 1800s. That's so long ago no one cares now," he said, hoping he sounded convincing. "And as for the so-called fortune, Lavita Wrenville never married, was eccentric and may have saved some money and hidden it, but she was considered by most to be poverty stricken after she went through the money left to her by her father. All I've ever heard was that she lived in poverty and off other people's charity."

"Maybe you're too closely involved," Destiny said lightly, her constant smiles softening her persistent argument with him. "I find that it's still an interesting subject and I hope I can persuade you to give me an interview. I would be absolutely thrilled," she said in a throaty voice that made him think of hot kisses instead of a factual interview. "After all, you are a Milan and one of the men murdered in that house was a Milan—wasn't one of your ancestors rumored to have been murdered by a Calhoun?"

"Unfortunately, yes, that's my family's version, though the Calhouns say it was a Calhoun murdered by a Milan. But it was way before my time and I sure as hell didn't know him. There's not that much to talk about. Later in her life, Lavita Wrenville was considered a recluse and an eccentric old maid. End of information."

"Sheriff Milan, I hope it's not the end of information or our conversations. I imagine you know all sorts of things, maybe more than anyone else, about history here." She rewarded him with another dazzling smile that made him want to stop arguing with her. "I have been looking forward so much to meeting you."

He could see why Dwight didn't know how she had talked him into letting her wait in Wyatt's office. It was difficult to keep his mind on his subject with her hanging on his every word, smiling at him constantly and sounding as if she might be talking to the most brilliant man in Verity. That plus her looks probably caused her to get her way almost 100 percent of the time. Of their own will, his eyes glanced down at her long legs. Just looking at them sparked desire. He didn't want to give her an interview. He wanted to seduce her and then send her on her way.

"Maybe I can get you to change your mind about the interview," she said in a breathy voice.

"You can try," he replied with amusement.

"I think that will be a fun project."

He found himself excited by the challenge. Yes, it was going to be difficult to say no to Destiny Jones.

With an effort he looked up again. He gazed into the green eyes that held him captive. His every nerve sizzled, his pulse quickened and his breathing altered. He wanted to reach for her and close the last bit of distance between them even though he knew this whole conversation was to get what she wanted from him.

"Sheriff Milan," she drawled.

With an effort he sat straighter. "No interview," he gasped, struggling to get his voice back to normal while fighting the urge to lean the last few inches and kiss her.

She smiled. "I hope you'll change your mind. You're part of this town and one of families involved in the famous feud and you're sheriff—there would be a lot of interest."

"I lead a quiet life. I don't think I would be that interesting and the feud is fading, so I don't care to bring it back into the limelight."

She laughed, a sunny, contagious, merry sound that he could listen to all day. His mind groped for sanity and to get back to a factual, impersonal conversation. He felt as if he wanted to loosen his collar. Even more, he wanted to reach for her, to kiss that full mouth and feel her softness pressed against him. Lost in that mental picture, he struggled to remember what he had to discuss with her.

"Your limo is in my parking place and you have a ticket," he blurted in an effort to get back to business. His voice came out with a husky note and it was difficult to think about business or anything except giving in to her or kissing her. He didn't like that loss of control. He didn't give in to his urges anymore, not after getting his heart broken by Katherine. "We've called to have the limo towed," he said, beginning to gather his wits. "Where's your driver?"

"I told him I'd call him when I'm through talking to you. He's just looking at the town or getting coffee. He's not far."

"You need to get that limo moved now," Wyatt declared, barely aware of what he said to her, also barely noticing that she had no reaction to his announcement that her limo would be towed.

"Oh, he will as soon as I'm finished here. I can be persistent, Sheriff Milan, when I want something," she said. "I want to try to change your mind. You do change your mind sometimes, don't you?" She asked in such a friendly, good-natured tone, he had to laugh.

"Yes, I can change my mind," he replied, thinking she was the biggest challenge he had had in too long to remember. He couldn't recall ever being so totally distracted. "Are you staying in Verity tonight, or somewhere else?" he said, knowing her answer but hoping for a different one.

"My staff and I are staying in the Verity Hotel."

"A good place to stay. The Verity Hotel doesn't have any unsolved mysteries or even ancient legends, but it's an old hotel dating back to 1887. It burned in the early 1900s and was rebuilt. It has been remodeled several times including in 2002, as well as in the past three years when it was completely renovated. It's a nice place to stay."

As he talked, he continued to study her, struggling to drag his attention elsewhere. Her movie star, younger sister was breathtakingly beautiful, far more flirty, but Destiny was a combination of friendly charm and sensuality, a sexual appeal that set his pulse pounding. He suspected his reaction was generally same as it was with every man she encountered.

"Did Mayor Nash tell you the history of Verity or the Wrenville house?"

"No," she said. "He merely welcomed me to town and seemed happy that I had an interest in using the Wrenville house for one of my subjects. I have an appointment with him later this week."

Wyatt wanted to say, *I'll bet you do.* Instead, different words came out of his mouth. "Since you don't know our history, let me take you to dinner tonight and I'll tell you about it." The words just popped out as if he had no control over what he said. For his own good he should get rid of this woman and avoid her as much as possible. Instead, he had invited her out. And dammit, he could not keep from hoping she would accept.

"How delightful," she said, smiling again. "Thank you. I would love to go to dinner with you and hear about your life, Verity and the Wrenville house. I can send my limo to pick you up."

Her words lifted the fog that had settled on his brain. Smiling, he shook his head. "Thanks. I'll come to the hotel and get you. Seven?"

"Fine," she said, standing and offering her hand.

He wrapped his fingers around hers, stepping closer to her at the same time. She didn't step back, but instead continued to smile as she looked up at him. He was within inches, his hand holding hers, sending streaks of fire from the simple physical contact. She had a lush body made for love, and tonight, he intended to take her to dinner and afterward, to seduce her. And he hoped she would be willing in an effort to get what she wanted from him.

"It's been interesting," he said in a husky voice.

"But you wish I'd go away," she said, softening her words with another one of her fabulous smiles.

"I didn't say that I didn't like you. You're big city—

we're small town," he said in a husky voice. "Charming, stunning and captivating."

"Thank you, Sheriff Milan. How nice you are."

"It's Wyatt. I have a feeling we'll see each other often while you're here," he said, wondering if she would be as enticing to kiss as he thought she might be.

"We'll see each other," she said, the breathless note returning to her voice. "I think hierarchy is on my side on this one. The governor of Texas trumps the sheriff of Verity. I came prepared. My sister has told me about you in great detail."

He merely smiled, recalling how angry her sister had been with him the last hour they had spent together. She had wanted him to go back to California with her and she was accustomed to getting her way. When he had refused, it did not go well. If she'd planned to stay, he'd have broken up with her, but since she was leaving Verity forever, he played the affair to its end, even though he had grown tired of her and her appeal had fizzled.

He suspected her older sister was just as stubborn. In spite of Destiny's smiles and polite charm, he continually felt their clash of wills.

He dropped her hand and headed to the door. As she walked beside him, he inhaled the scent of her mesmerizing perfume. He opened his office door and they walked out into the reception area where a group had gathered. Cameras flashed while people clamored noisily as they surged toward her.

Wyatt stepped in front of her, shielding her from the reporters that he easily recognized, two local, the others from the area and one from a Fort Worth station and one from Dallas. His deputy came forward to help, but Destiny stepped easily in front of Wyatt.

"I'll be happy to answer your questions," she said, smiling at the media.

"Not in here, please," Wyatt said in an authoritative tone that caused a hush. "Folks, take the interview across the street. We have to conduct business here, not a press conference. Jeff, Millie, Duncan—outside, please," Wyatt said, calling the names of the reporters that had the most influence. He knew nearly everyone in the crowd.

"We'll go across the street," Destiny said, smiling at the crowd and shaking someone's outstretched hand.

Wyatt watched a man and a woman emerge from the crowd. He didn't know them, but they flanked Destiny and he guessed they were two of her staff members.

"Dammit," he said quietly, thinking about Destiny putting the Wrenville house—and, as a result, the Milans, the Calhouns and their feud—on television for the world to view. He didn't think it would be any easier to keep her out of the Wrenville house than to get her out of his parking spot.

"I'm going to see Gyp," he said tersely to his deputy.

He shook his head. "The mayor left for the day. He said to tell you he would see you in the morning."

"Dammit," Wyatt repeated, turning to go back into his office, figuring Gyp had ducked out on him because he knew Wyatt would be unhappy. Wyatt shook his head as he swore again. Townspeople would not be thrilled when Destiny Jones fanned the flames of old animosities.

Abruptly, Wyatt headed out the back door of city hall, circling to Main Street in long strides, hoping the limo was gone and her impromptu press conference was over. As he turned the corner, he stopped short. Not only was the red limo still in his parking place, but her audience had grown. In addition, a TV truck was parked down the street, lights had been set up and he could see men with video cameras. Shaking his head, Wyatt stared at the circus going on across the street. The lady knew how to draw a crowd. He made a mental note to get a private room for their dinner.

Wyatt scanned the crowd that spilled into the street and lined the sidewalk. He recognized Dustin Redwing and Pete Lee, two men who worked for him. He saw the curly white hair of Horace Pringle, the president of Verity's largest bank. Ty Hemmings, the owner of the movie theater, was in the audience, along with several other shop owners. He spotted Farley White, his mechanic.

Wyatt knew nearly everyone in the gathering. He shook his head at the sight of Charlie Akin, the local eccentric who lived in a shack along the river in a neighboring county. Periodically, the river flooded, taking Charlie's shack. He moved downriver or upriver, staying in the general area and built another shack, taking his goats and chickens with him. Wyatt wondered how Charlie had gotten word that Destiny Jones was in Verity.

Deputy Lambert stood nearby, watching the crowd, and Wyatt was certain his deputy was there out of a sense of duty. Wyatt continued studying the crowd, recognizing face after face, being only slightly surprised that Destiny had drawn such a gathering because she would draw attention wherever she went.

He looked at her as she answered a question. A breeze tugged long tendrils of her deep auburn hair. She looked like a movie star standing there in the sunshine while people asked her questions. She glanced his way. Even though he knew it was ridiculous, he felt as if she had reached out and touched him. Her gaze held his while she finished her answer. Then she turned to look at someone asking her a question.

His cell phone rang and he pulled it out to see he had a text from his brother Nick. "Dammit," Wyatt said quietly, scanning Nick's text.

SARA ORWIG 23

Watching Destiny Jones in Verity on TV. Why didn't you let us know? When can I meet her? How long will she be in Verity? The Wrenville murders?

As he read it he received another text, this one from his youngest brother, Tony, also wanting to know about Destiny. Wyatt shook his head and strode through the front door of city hall.

"Sheriff," Dwight said, shaking his head, "Argus is dealing with two wrecked cars on the highway and he can't tow the limo for several hours."

"Okay. Val is across the street. Do you know if he found the driver?"

"He did. The man said he would move the limo when his boss told him to move it."

Wyatt smiled and shook his head again. Was she doing this deliberately to get his attention? Beneath her smiles and charm was a strong will. He shook his head and went to his office to call Nick first on his private line.

"Nick, you have too many questions for a text. I didn't know she was coming. Yes, I've met her. I don't know about introducing you, but are you sure you want to meet her?"

"You've got to be kidding. Look at the crowd she's drawn. If you didn't know she was coming, then the town didn't know," Nick replied.

"I think that's right."

"She knows how to draw a crowd."

"All she has to do is walk down the street."

"Amen. You've got that right. Try to figure some way we can meet her. Tony's already sent me a text. How come you're not out there?"

"I've already met her, and my deputy is there."

"So you've talked to her."

"A little. I'll get you the introduction, and I'll call you about when and where."

"Thanks, Wyatt. She said she's staying at the Verity Hotel."

"So she told everyone, including the press, where she'll be. The lady does want attention. Don't tell me you're going to hang out in the lobby?"

Nick chuckled. "Hardly. No, I'll meet her, but not that way. Thanks for calling."

"I'll keep in touch."

Wyatt sent Tony a text. Three minutes later his phone rang.

"I'm watching Destiny Jones in Verity on TV."

"I'm sure you are. I've talked to Nick and I promise I'll introduce both of you sometime."

"Cool. Don't forget. Right now you're missing her interview."

"I'll live. Talk to you soon, Tony." Wyatt picked up an iPad from his desk and switched to the television cable to pick up her interview. He watched her deftly field questions, give answers that would bring laughter and generally captivate the audience. He gazed at her green eyes and auburn hair. It wouldn't matter if she had mumbled and had nothing to say. She was gorgeous and charming and her audience was enchanted.

Wyatt's jaw clamped shut a little more tightly as he listened to her talk about wanting to learn about Lavita Wrenville and how fascinating Verity's history was, including the Milan-Calhoun feud. Each minute he watched her his hopes sank lower because at dinner he had hoped to discourage her from using the unsolved murders at the Wrenville house for a show. There would be no way, now that she'd spoken about it to the media, that she'd pack up and go back to Chicago.

He thought about her parking the red limo in his space. That had not been a casual, thoughtless event. She wanted the town's attention and she had known exactly what she was doing then, just as she knew what she was doing now in talking to the crowd that was still growing. Shortly, he would have to go out there and break it up because they would be blocking traffic on Main if many more people came to watch her.

Even as he thought that and watched, she told the crowd farewell. A man stepped in front of her and a woman moved on one side of her. To Wyatt's surprise Val moved beside her on the other side as a second woman fell in behind them. They crossed the street, the man in the lead clearing the way while a smaller crowd flowed with her. When they reached the red limo, the man leading the way held the door. She turned to smile and wave at the crowd, thanking them, throwing them a kiss and then vanishing into the limo, followed by the two women, the tinted windows hiding the interior. In seconds the limo slowly eased from the curb and the crowd dispersed.

He switched off the iPad and stood, rubbing the back of his neck.

He had mixed feelings about dinner with her, but his desire to spend the evening with her outweighed his dislike of having to deal with her about the Wrenville murders and the old family feud. Seven o'clock couldn't come too soon.

Wyatt nodded. This might be a night to remember.

Two

Destiny and her staff entered the hotel and took the VIP elevator to the top floor where she had all four suites. In addition to hers, Virginia and Duke Boyden, her camera operator and her chauffeur, shared a suite, while Amy had her own suite next to Destiny's.

Destiny entered her suite, followed by Amy Osgood, her cousin and assistant. Destiny barely glanced at a huge bouquet of pink-and-white lilies on the oval glass table in front of the sofa. Amy paused beside a large round platter holding cheeses, crackers and fruit. A stack of china plates and cutlery was on a tray next to the hors d'oeuvres. Amy picked up a card. "Compliments of the Verity Hotel," she read.

"Take all that to your room. I really don't want any of it."

"Thanks, Destiny. I'll take some. I have a smaller version in my room and the Boydens have one, also."

"Y'all can share mine," Destiny said as she tossed aside

her large bag. She was remembering the moment in his office that Sheriff Wyatt Milan had entered. The most vivid, crystal-blue eyes she had ever seen had taken her breath away, holding her immobile, stopping her thoughts while they had stared at each other. She had seen pictures of him, but she wasn't prepared for the man in person. No wonder Desirée had fallen for him. She had never understood what had gotten into her little sister to go to some tiny town in Texas and fall head over heels in love with the sheriff.

She had learned soon enough that she had been wrong in her views of the small Texas town. Verity's residents had enormous wealth. She had been surprised when she had learned the sheriff himself was a billionaire rancher, a member of an old-time Texas family, a former professional football player and he held a law degree. But looking into his blue eyes today, feeling the force of his personality when he had simply entered the room, she realized why Desirée had been bowled over. The man was larger-than-life. One look and her opinions of Wyatt Milan had changed instantly.

Wavy brown hair above a face with rugged features, prominent cheekbones, a slight bump in his nose, maybe from a break, a stubborn jut to his chin. He wore a neat brown uniform with an unofficial hand-tooled leather belt around his narrow waist and boots on his feet. It wouldn't have mattered what he wore; just standing quietly he had a commanding presence.

She spun around in a circle with her arms outstretched. "Congratulate me, Amy. Sheriff Milan is taking me to dinner tonight. Just what I want, but coming sooner than I expected."

"Congratulations!" Amy said, glancing at her boss with a frown.

"Don't look so worried."

"You said he doesn't want you here or want you using Verity for a show," Amy said.

"Sheriff Milan will change his mind. You'll see. Besides, I have the letter from the governor of Texas and a letter from Mayor Nash."

"So when are you going to make it public that you have a tie to this town?" Amy asked.

"I told you—when I can get the most attention by doing so. Attention for the show. I'll make my announcement when I'm taping. Until then it's our little secret. Verity doesn't make the news, so it's never been picked up by the media that I have a connection here."

"Sheriff Milan already isn't happy with you. He'll really dislike learning your mother is in a branch of the Calhoun family from here."

Destiny smiled. "We'll see when the time comes. Until then—bury it."

"I will. It's a shame the sheriff doesn't want you here. I think the story of the murders should be interesting. People in the crowd today seemed to like you and want you here."

"Verity is a small town and they keep to themselves. No one has ever made an issue about the house or publicized it. It's just gone unnoticed. Lots of towns that have something like this capitalize on it and make it a tourist attraction or Halloween event and get attention, but not here. That makes it good for me to use in my book whether or not I find anything. I don't really expect to solve the old murders. It's been more than a hundred years since Lavita Wrenville's demise."

"You must have made an impression on Sheriff Milan since he asked you to dinner tonight."

"He invited me to dinner to try to talk me out of staying here and doing a show about the Wrenville house. He doesn't know that I've heard about the murders, the legend and the feud from Mimi," she said, using the name she had called her grandmother since she had learned to talk

"Your grandmother seems to know a lot about this town even though she never lived here."

"She lived in Dallas and had other Calhoun relatives here. She's the one who interested me in the story of Lavita Wrenville and the triple murders."

"It will shock people when you announce you're a Calhoun," Amy said and Destiny smiled. "It will add a little spice to the story of the Wrenville murders. I hope it doesn't rock the sheriff too badly."

Amy continued, "I heard a woman broke their engagement and Sheriff Milan hasn't had a serious affair since. That might explain his actions with your sister. He's about the only one who had an affair with her and didn't propose."

"So he's had a broken heart? Interesting," Destiny said, thinking about Wyatt. "I don't think Desirée knew that, but she's more interested in herself than the men she dates, so she doesn't really learn a lot about them. Wyatt keeps himself all buttoned up. He likes women—and vice versa, I'm sure. Desirée probably did what every other single female in this town has done—fallen in love with him. Have you ever seen such blue eyes?"

"I haven't met him yet. I think he stood across the street today when you talked to all the people."

"Yes, he did. Did any of you find out why our billionaire rancher is also sheriff of Verity? Mimi knew nothing about that."

"Actually, from what we've pieced together it's because of the Wrenville house."

Destiny stopped looking through her purse and raised her head. "How so?" She held up her hand. "Wait. I better get ready for tonight. He's picking me up at seven. Come tell me while I decide what to wear." She headed into the large bedroom. A huge bouquet of red anthurium and purple gladioli stood on a table. She glanced at the card. "Enjoy your stay. Verity Chamber of Commerce."

Amy went on to explain what they'd learned. "All we could find out is that next year the Wrenville house reverts totally to the town and the town officials can do what they want with the house and property. The people wanted someone for sheriff they could trust when that happens and by general consensus, Wyatt Milan is a trustworthy and honest man, so they talked him into running for office."

"And he's probably not happy with someone—me—coming in and poking around before he has control," Destiny added.

"Everyone seems to like him as sheriff."

"Especially the ladies, I imagine. According to Desirée, men like him, too." Destiny looked through her clothes. "About tonight, did you let some of the press know that I'm going out with Sheriff Milan?"

"Yes, I did."

"Good. I'm going to shower. And I'll make a call to Mimi and to Desirée."

"If you don't need anything else right now, I'll go unpack some more of my things."

"Thanks for doing mine earlier."

"Sure," Amy said over her shoulder as she left the suite.

Destiny showered, then pulled on undergarments and a robe and got her iPad to do FaceTime with her grandmother. She felt better if she could see the frail, aging woman. Destiny settled back to talk, waiting patiently because it took time for her grandmother to deal with Face-Time.

"Mimi, I've met Sheriff Milan," she said after inquiring about her grandmother's health and listening to her talk about her day.

"Did he take it well to discover you're a Calhoun? Desirée never told him she was," Mimi said. "Then again Desirée can barely remember her heritage and really doesn't care."

"I haven't told him yet either. I'm waiting for the perfect moment. He's taking me to dinner tonight."

"He's a Milan, Destiny. You can't trust a Milan."

"Mimi, I think I can trust this one. He got elected sheriff because everyone in Verity trusts him, even Calhouns. Besides, tonight is a business dinner. He wants to talk me out of putting Verity on my show."

"Pay no attention," her white-haired grandmother said, smiling. "He's a Milan and they're hardheaded and I still say he probably won't give you straight answers."

Destiny held back a laugh. Her grandmother never even lived in Verity and knew about the feud only from her parents and grandparents, yet she harbored strong feelings against the Milans. She was the one who had told Destiny of her Calhoun genealogy.

"I'll let you know how it went," Destiny said, moving to other subjects until finally, she told her grandmother she needed to go.

"Take care of yourself, Destiny. If the sheriff doesn't want you there, maybe you should reconsider. Please be careful."

"I'll be careful. I love you, Mimi," she said. "Call me anytime," she added, wishing she could do more to make her grandmother comfortable, knowing her arthritis bothered her and she didn't get enough sleep at night.

She thought about the tall, ruggedly appealing sheriff of Verity and her pulse quickened. This would be more interesting than she had anticipated. And more challenging. Most men she encountered were struck by her looks and eager to please her. Wyatt Milan was an exception, but she enjoyed a challenge.

Desirée had told Destiny if she wanted cooperation from the sheriff, she should flirt with him and resort to her fe-

male wiles to get what she wanted. He might be happy with
some flirting, but Destiny didn't think it would change his
opinion one bit. It certainly hadn't worked with her sister. He'd been one of the few men able to resist Desirée.

Desirée had gotten over Wyatt and he was all but forgotten within a month after she returned to California.
She could forget men as easily as she fell in love with
them. Now that Destiny knew Wyatt, she wondered why
her sister had ever thought he would go with her back to
California. She could, however, understand why Desirée
had been attracted to him.

She crossed the room to look in the closet again to decide what she would wear, finally selecting a dress that
she hoped would get Wyatt's attention.

At five before seven she critically studied her image in
the full-length mirror, trying to decide if she had achieved
the look she wanted. The straight black dress hugged her
curves from her waist down, and the top of the dress had
a one-shoulder neckline in hot pink that matched her high-
heeled sandals. Her hair was pinned up, with curly strands
falling free around her face. Gold earrings dangled from
her ears and along with the gold bracelets complemented
her gold necklace with three diamonds centered in it.

Satisfied with her appearance, she picked up a small
black purse just as the phone rang and she answered to
hear Wyatt's voice saying he was in the lobby.

Since she had told the media why she was in Verity, she
expected to get attention all the time she was in town.
When she stepped down into the lobby from the curving
staircase from the mezzanine, she noticed two men with
cameras aimed at her. In fact, every man in the lobby
looked in her direction. Her pulse skipped a beat when
she spotted Wyatt Milan. Dressed in a charcoal suit, black
boots, a black wide-brimmed hat, he stood a few yards
from the bottom step.

His gaze met hers, causing her heart to thud. Smiling at him, she walked down the stairs. She was aware of the cameras, but her gaze was on Wyatt, who looked back with the faintest hint of a smile.

At the bottom step he came forward. "Destiny," he said, the simple pronunciation of her name sounding different from anyone else she had heard say it. She tingled from her head to her toes. She'd never had a physical reaction to a man as intense as with Wyatt. She had never expected to be so attracted to him. His electronic pictures had not conveyed his appeal.

He gave her a full smile, laugh lines creasing the corners of his mouth, and she actually felt weak in the knees as he linked her arm with his.

A man holding a camera stepped close. "Evening, Wyatt. Ms. Jones, I'm Carl Stanley with the Verity paper. Is Sheriff Milan taking you to the Wrenville house now?"

"I didn't dress this way to go to the Wrenville house," she said, laughing along with Carl and the others around her. "That will come a little later," she answered, smiling at him.

"How did you hear about Verity and the Wrenville house? Was it from your sister when she visited?"

"I heard about it before that. Maybe Verity is more famous than people who live here realize," she said while the reporter took notes.

"Do you hope to solve the mystery of the three murders in Lavita's house?"

"That would be a fabulous result, but I don't expect to get answers to questions that people have been asking for over a century. We're just looking into the situation. Sometimes my show, *Unsolved Mysteries,* prompts people to come forward. We've had some solutions to puzzling cases since we started the series."

"Are you going to interview local people for your show?"

"Carl, in due time you'll see how the show unfolds. Thank you for your questions and your interest. Verity is one of the friendliest towns I've ever visited. We'll talk again," Destiny said, smiling as he raised his digital camera and got a close-up of her. Two more men moved closer and she smiled and posed while they took pictures.

Wyatt stepped forward. "Okay, guys, you have your pictures. We'll be going now. Ms. Jones will be around to answer questions later this week." He whisked her outside and into a black sports car. In long strides he circled the car and climbed inside to drive away.

"You handled that well," she said.

"I believe you're the one who handled it. You're news right now and they're interested, which you expected them to be, and I can't blame them. This is a quiet town."

She laughed softly. "Are they following us?"

"No, they won't follow us. Sorry if you're disappointed."

"Why are you so certain they won't follow?"

"They know me and they know I don't want them trailing after me. They want my cooperation too often to cross me."

"So what if someone does?" she persisted.

"We'll see. It hasn't ever happened."

"I don't think I'm the only one here who's accustomed to getting his way."

The corner of Wyatt's mouth lifted slightly, but he didn't glance her way or answer and they rode a few minutes in silence.

"Am I really the first outside person to show an interest in the Wrenville house?" Destiny asked. "That's what someone told me."

"As far as I know. I can't really speak for before my time." He checked his mirrors. "My deputy and I stayed out there once, just to see if anything happened or if vagrants were in there. Nothing happened and no one was staying there. The house is run-down, neglected. No one's lived in it since the 1800s. It was well built to begin with or it would be falling in by now, but when something is abandoned, it doesn't last."

"So the house is ignored by one and all."

"That sums it up. I think you'll have a difficult time filling half an hour about the house or the people who died in it."

"We'll see. I hope you'll consider a brief interview. Since you're a Milan, I think it would be of interest."

"Sorry, the answer's still the same. No interview. So far, no occasion has ever arisen in Verity that warrants an interview from me, other than just answering brief questions for the news. And that's the way I hope it remains. I wouldn't be that interesting, anyway."

"I differ on that topic. I'm not accustomed to getting turned down."

Wyatt gave her a quick glance. "I'm sure that's the truth. I imagine you're accustomed to getting what you want from men."

"Most of the time, I do. So far, you're proving to be an exception, but I hope I can change your mind."

He glanced over at her. "It all depends on what you want from me," he said, a husky note coming into his voice that gave her the satisfaction of knowing he had some kind of reaction to her.

"Wyatt," she said, "you haven't discouraged me. I still hope to get an interview from you. I know it would be interesting."

"You'd be surprised how dull I can get. Ask a local reporter. Their eyes glaze over sometimes, but it shortens interviews."

She laughed softly again. "I don't think you really do

that—at least I would guess it is rare. I'm still going for an interview of my own." She received another glance and this time his crystal-blue eyes darkened slightly and the look he gave her raised the temperature in the car.

"You go ahead and try," he said in a deep voice that made her heart race.

"So that doesn't scare you?" she asked.

"Hardly. It'll be interesting to see you bargain for an interview," he replied. He shook his head. "The evening has definitely taken a turn for the better."

"We'll see," she replied.

Leaning back in the seat, she gave thought to the situation. Wyatt wasn't reacting to her the way the majority of men did. She had grown up knowing that she was not the pretty daughter in her family. Desirée was breathtakingly beautiful and had been so all her life. Destiny had unruly red hair, was tall, but not stunning in her physical appearance, especially during her awkward teen years, but from an early age, she had learned to please and charm those around her to get what she wanted. With her relatives, she had poured out her love, being cooperative, obedient, helpful and turning on the sweetness when she needed to. During her later teens with boys her age, she had flirted, and it hadn't taken much to melt them into hopeful males eager to please her.

It shocked her that, so far, Wyatt had resisted her smiles and easy requests.

She studied his profile, the firm jaw, prominent cheekbones, a slight bump near the bridge of his nose. He was not what she had expected and she was having a reaction to him that surprised and disturbed her.

"Do you have other places in Texas that you'll visit?" he asked.

"Not at this time."

As she watched him drive, he gave her a quick glance. "So how is Desirée?" he asked.

"She's fine. She recently married."

"I saw that she did. I hope she's very happy."

"I'll tell her you said that."

"Does she know you're in Verity?"

"Yes, she does. From what I hear, you're still single, which surprises me."

"Now why would that surprise you?" he asked.

"You're handsome, in your early thirties, appealing, influential and well-known. I'm sure every female in this county knows you. If we consider just the single ladies, I'd guess the ones in this county plus the next three or four counties know you. Texas women are beautiful. The elements are right for you to fall in love and marry."

He smiled without taking his attention from the road. "You'd think, but it hasn't happened."

"So there's no one you had to explain to about taking me to dinner tonight?"

"No, there isn't. By the way, while you're here, two of my brothers want to meet you. They saw you on TV today, and one of them has read your last book."

"Well, I'm happy to discuss my book with anyone who is interested," she replied. "So my book is why they want to meet me?"

"Not altogether," Wyatt replied. "It's part of the reason. I imagine every man in Verity would like to meet you. And maybe every male over fifteen in the next four or five counties," he said.

"I take it your brothers are single."

"One is widowed and the other is my single, youngest brother, so you're right. Nick lost his pregnant wife. He's still hurting pretty badly. It's been a rough time for him and he's not dating anyone."

"I'm sorry to hear that," she said, startled about the loss in Wyatt's family. "I don't think Desirée knew that."

"There's no reason for her to keep up with Nick, and that hadn't happened when she was here."

Destiny gazed out the window, taken aback once again by seeing a more serious side to Wyatt. Now that she was getting to know him a little, she wanted to be more up-front with him and thought about the right moment to reveal her genealogy. "Well, I, for one, have been curious about you. There aren't many men who can upset my sister."

"I'm sorry if I did, but I don't think it was devastating since she was married within the year—I believe her first marriage. In the three years since we dated, isn't this marriage number two? I don't think she's been pining away over me."

"Perhaps not. It's too bad. Now that I've met you, I imagine you would have had a settling influence on her. A sheriff, rock solid, mid-America, a Texan. How the two of you got together in the first place, I can't imagine," she added. "You don't look the type to be knocked off your feet simply because she's a movie star."

"You have that much right," he said, smiling again. "Look again at your sister. She's one of the most beautiful women I've ever seen. You're one of the most stunning. And she flirts outrageously, which I'm sure you already know."

"Thank you. My sister is beautiful. She's been beautiful from the day she was born." After a moment of silence, Destiny turned to him. "You were rather laid-back today. Do you ever get upset, Sheriff?"

"Sure, when things get bad enough. Most of the time in Verity, there's nothing bad enough."

"So my reporting about the Wrenville house murders isn't bad enough to get you riled up?"

"Not so far," he said. "Maybe your quest is annoying, but not critical. We'll see as time goes by."

She saw that the buildings on Main Street had given way to houses. Heading east, they passed two blocks of wooden Victorian-style homes, some single story, some two or three stories with tall trees that had thick trunks in what looked like an old part of town.

"We have passed most of Verity's restaurants. Where are we going?"

"To the airport. We'll fly to Dallas to eat. You have no objection to that, do you?"

"Of course not," she said. "So you'll avoid the press for the rest of the night."

"I sure hope so," he replied, "and I hope that doesn't disappoint you."

"If it did, I don't think you'd turn around and go back," she said, amused. "So the sheriff of Verity has his own plane. Interesting."

"Actually, it's mutually owned by me and my siblings. We all have ranches and want to be able to come and go, so we bought two planes and hired pilots and the necessary employees. I have my own pilot's license, as do my brothers Nick and Tony. It's worked out great."

"Nice, if you can afford it." She looked out at the passing scenery. "I recall we came into town this way so we should be passing the Wrenville house. There it is," she said, looking at a wooden three-story home surrounded by a three-foot wrought-iron fence and a front gate hanging on one hinge. She noticed several of the windows had been broken out.

"Just an old, empty house that the town will own shortly," Wyatt said. "Nothing exciting there. And there can't be any clues in it about the three men who died there."

"You don't discourage me. It's more interesting than that." Destiny said, taking in the weeds and high grass that filled the yard while the two tall oaks by the house were overgrown with vines. "No, I'm excited, filled with curiosity. Sometimes it's surprising what my show stirs up. Maybe someone will come forth with information that has been passed down through the generations. A Milan and a Calhoun both in love with the same woman and both shot dead over her, along with her father—that's an interesting unsolved mystery. You have to admit it."

"Interesting to an outsider, I suppose, but we don't need the old feud stirred up. As generations pass it has weakened and with my generation, I think the feud is dying. I want it to die. We're a quiet little town. I don't want to see that disturbed needlessly."

"A quiet little town with a high percentage of millionaires," she said. She realized she had never known anyone as protective of his hometown and his family and she had to respect Wyatt for that.

"West Texas is good cattle and oil country, plus a few other businesses that have done well here," he replied.

In minutes he turned along a narrow asphalt road and shortly she saw two hangars and a control tower ahead. A jet was outside and she assumed it would be the plane they would take to Dallas.

Wyatt picked up his phone to talk to his pilot, letting him know they were almost there, and she tingled with anticipation, looking forward to an evening with Wyatt Milan. She wondered what he would think when he learned she was a Calhoun. He acted as if he thought the old feud should die, but she barely knew him. When it involved him personally, would he still think the feud should end? Mimi had painted such a dark picture of the Milans as dishonest, crafty and manipulative that Destiny had expected a man far different from the Milan she was getting to know tonight. None of those descriptions fit Wyatt. Far from it. Honest, straightforward, hoping for good—he embodied admirable qualities. She loved Mimi and they were close, but her grandmother was wrong about this Milan.

Her gaze lowered to his mouth. Strong, firm, his lips made her wonder if he would kiss her tonight. The chemistry between them was exciting. She felt it, and she was certain he did, too. Could she kiss him into agreeing to an interview?

Three

As they reached the plane, Wyatt stopped near a brown-haired man with touches of gray in his hair. He smiled at Destiny.

"Destiny, meet our pilot, Jason Whittaker. Jason, this is Ms. Jones from Chicago."

"It's Destiny," she said, offering her hand. "I'm happy to meet you and looking forward to the flight."

"Unsolved Mysteries," Jason said and Destiny's smile broadened. Wyatt watched her step forward and charm his pilot who could not take his gaze from her. Wyatt could understand. She'd stolen his breath when she had appeared at the top of the stairs at the hotel. The woman knew how to make a grand entrance. Every man in the hotel lobby had been watching her and Wyatt had heard an audible sigh from several who were standing near him when she appeared. She wasn't the delicate, perfect beauty her sister was. Instead, she was hot, sexual, lush, with a voluptuous body, a come-hither look and unruly red hair that

looked as if she had just left a romp in bed. How was he going to keep denying her an interview or discouraging her from the Wrenville house? She left him tongue-tied, on fire, unable to think clearly, torn between wanting to seduce her and hoping she would pack up and go. Never had a woman rocked him like this one.

"We have good weather," the pilot remarked, pulling Wyatt from his reverie.

"Let's get going," Wyatt said, taking her arm and boarding the plane. The moment he touched her, the casual contact electrified him. Her perfume deepened his awareness of her at his side. He motioned to a seat and as she sat near a window and buckled herself in, he sat facing her.

She looked out the window and the plane began to taxi away from the hangar. When they were airborne and headed southeast, she turned to Wyatt.

"So tell me the history of the Lavita Wrenville house."

"In the early days Verity was a hub for cattle ranchers. The Wrenville family was successful and built their big home. Lavita's father still had eastern interests and was partners with his brother in a large bank in Boston. At one time, according to legend or family history, the Wrenvilles were enormously wealthy—in a time and place where there were an unusually high number of wealthy families."

"The Milans and the Calhouns included, right?"

"Yes. According to local history, the Milans made a fortune with cattle and ranching. I guess that's where I get my love of ranching. So did the Calhouns. From the earliest days, I think the Calhouns and Milans clashed over land, cattle, water, running the town, all sorts of reasons, including the women they loved, so the feud started."

"I think I'm getting the short version of Milan and Wrenville history."

"You're getting the only version I have," he remarked.

"Sorry, I interrupted you. Go ahead."

"As local history goes, the Wrenvilles gradually amassed more money than anyone else in town. Hubert Wrenville had cattle, land, the big bank, the feed store, the biggest saloon."

"Was this Lavita's father?"

"Yes. Finally, there was only Lavita Wrenville who lived alone in the house. She was an eccentric old maid who did not want anyone to inherit or buy the house. Lavita deeded the property, house, stable, outbuildings and all personal property in those buildings to Verity with the stipulation that the property is not to be sold or changed until next year. At that time the Wrenville property and everything on it will revert totally to Verity to do with as it pleases. I imagine the town will sell the property if they can. That's what is in Lavita's official will and she was the last surviving Wrenville."

"Ah, I see. So what about information regarding the murders or a fortune she amassed and hid somewhere in the house?"

"I think that's just rumors, legend, wishful thinking of people way back and handed down through generations. There's nothing in the will about either one."

"Interesting," she said. "Maybe I'll do a show on Lavita Wrenville and the unsolved killings and then come back next year."

"You might consider just coming then. I don't think you'll find much of interest now. I've just told you everything about it. I don't think there's a fortune or a letter that revealed what happened."

"Suppose I search and find a fortune and a letter revealing what happened the night of the murders?"

"You wouldn't be the first to search. But there's nothing in her will about a fortune or a letter. That's legend."

"You really don't want me here, do you?" she asked, smiling slightly.

He leaned close, looking into her big green eyes that widened. "Oh, yes, I want you here. I have plans for tonight. From the moment I walked into my office and saw you, I've wanted you here," he said in a husky tone that was barely above a whisper.

She leaned in a fraction, so close they were almost touching, and he fought the urge to close the distance and kiss her. "Then we should have an interesting evening because I've been looking forward to tonight since we parted this afternoon," she whispered. Her words were slow, sultry, increasing the sexual tension between them. As they gazed at each other, again he was hot, tied in knots with desire, yet at the same time aware of the clash of wills between them.

She smiled and sat back. "This should be an interesting evening."

"I'll admit, you're not like other women I've known."

"That's a relief," she said and he gave her a faint smile.

"Tell me about the murders. All I know is that Lavita's father, a Milan and a Calhoun all were shot to death."

Wyatt settled back, inhaled deeply and tried to get his wits about him. "All I've ever heard is that Lavita had two men in love with her—unfortunately, a Milan and a Calhoun. The feud had been in existence through at least two generations by then, so it was going strong and the two men did not speak to each other. The night of the shootings, they both called on her at the same time and neither would leave. She was upset. The men were angry and according to the old story, they were going to fight and pistols were drawn. Her father heard the argument, appeared and mixed in the struggle. Terrified what would happen, Lavita ran to get their stable keeper. As she rushed back to the house, shots were fired. According to the story, all three men were armed and had fired at each other, killing each other."

"So far, that's what I've been told."

"Some stories say that, on her deathbed, Lavita admitted that one of the men was still alive and conscious when she returned to the house and told Lavita what happened before he died. At the time of the murders, she had stated they were all dead by the time she got back."

"Couldn't the stable keeper verify her story?"

Wyatt smiled. "Remember, this was the late 1800s and the story has been passed down by word of mouth since. According to the story, the stable keeper went to get his pistol and was far enough behind Lavita that all three men were dead when he arrived at the scene. The three men died that night, presumably shortly after the shooting. And Lavita never revealed anyone talked to her until she was on her deathbed. Until then, she claimed she didn't know what had happened after she ran out of the house to get help."

"If that's the true story about what happened, it makes one wonder what she was told and why she hid it from the world. Nowadays, withholding information would put her behind bars."

"Early-day justice may have been dispensed differently and hers was an influential family. If the legend is true, she may not have wanted the true story to come out because of the feud. The Calhouns and the Milans had a history of getting revenge."

"This story holds possibilities for an interesting chapter in my next book."

Wyatt wanted to groan. He had hoped to discourage her with the story, which he found vague and probably hearsay. "It all comes down to trying to find an old letter Lavita wrote that reveals the truth about that night."

Destiny shifted in her seat, drawing his attention to her dress. The unique design left one shoulder bare. The other shoulder was covered by a short sleeve that had four buttons running down a center seam in the sleeve, so if unbuttoned, the front half of her dress would no longer be attached to the back half above the waist. The thought consumed him, distracting him from his story. He had to figuratively shake himself to get back on track.

"The letter has been rumored to be in the house," he continued. "I've never heard a version that included the grounds as a possibility," he added.

"Think there will be a bidding war on the property?"

"I don't. You never know what might appeal to a developer, but that property is in the industrial part of Verity, small as that is. In my view, it's far out for a likely shopping area. The town grew in all other directions. The house overlooks the cemetery on one side. The river runs behind it. Nearby is the airport and to the front is the highway. Not the greatest location. No one wanted the house and it was left to crumble." He sat back and crossed his leg over the other at the knee.

"Now that you know about it—and there is little to tell you—I hope you'll rethink using it on your show. The killings were long, long ago and of little interest," he said, watching her closely.

"I simply think you're trying to get rid of me," she replied sweetly, her green eyes sparkling. "The deaths of the three men are an interesting puzzle, plus the feud between two of them, two families who have many descendants today, you included."

"I suppose only the ratings will indicate which of us is right. There are far more intriguing unsolved mysteries in Texas. Come by the office and you can look at a list. It would be nice for all the residents if you would move on down the road."

"You're serious, aren't you?"

"Yes. I have a quiet, peaceful, pleasant town. The biggest problems this past year have been getting the Dixons' cat out of their chimney and getting Doc Lamon's dock back after it collapsed in a storm and floated downriver."

"When I talked to the group that gathered today, they were curious, interested and very friendly."

"They were curious, interested and friendly because you're a stunning, sexy woman. They were curious about you, not the old Wrenville place."

"Thank you. But I didn't get the feeling from any of them that someone would prefer that I didn't put Lavita Wrenville's story on my show. Did it occur to you that you might be wrong?"

"I know my town pretty well. I don't think I'm wrong," he said, knowing their quiet clash grew stronger and neither changed the other's opinion. "Today was a bunch of men who wanted to see you and talk to you. Wait until the women are involved and you're in Chicago and the results of your visit are right here in Verity for the locals to deal with. They won't be so happy or so cooperative, especially if you stir up that Milan-Calhoun feud."

"Have you always been right?"

"No, but I'm right often enough that I trust my own judgment."

She laughed and in spite of their steady battle, her stubborn refusal to leave Verity, her flagrant disregard for law in Verity, he wanted to wrap her in his arms and make love to her.

"It doesn't bother you that you're going to upset a whole town?"

"Of course it would bother me if I thought that would happen." She gave him an assessing look out of the corner of her eye. "It must be wonderful to feel you're always right."

He stifled a laugh and a retort

"Come by the office and look at that list of other unsolved Texas murders," he said, eliciting a smile from her. It seemed they had once again agreed to disagree.

Needing a break from his tenacious but beautiful opponent, he picked up the phone to confer with Jason on the arrival time. When he got his answer, he should have simply turned to look out the window but his eyes lit on Destiny instead. "No wedding ring," he observed. "So you're single."

"Definitely. There's no special man in my life at the moment."

"I'm glad to hear that since I'm taking you out."

"This wouldn't count anyway. You're taking me out to tell me about Lavita Wrenville and the unsolved murders. This is a business evening."

He leaned close again, placing his hands on the arms of her seat to hem her in while they gazed into each other's eyes. "There is no way this evening will be a business trip. The closest we'll come is the conversation we just had, and now I've finished giving you the Wrenville history. I've been looking forward to tonight all afternoon long."

"You want me to pack and return to Chicago and then you tell me you've been wanting to go out with me. That's contradictory," she said.

"My feelings are contradictory. You're a complication in my quiet life," he said, gazing into her big, green eyes that threatened to make him tell her to do whatever she wanted in Verity.

"A few complications in life sometimes make it more interesting. You'll be able to handle this one, I'm sure."

"I can't wait," he said, his heart drumming. He knew she wasn't going to leave quietly and she would be a constant challenge to him. The most enticing challenge he had ever had in his life.

As Destiny walked to a waiting limo, Wyatt took her arm and in minutes they were headed into downtown Dallas. Wyatt sat across from her, looking totally relaxed, his booted foot resting on his other knee, his hand on the arm of the seat. In spite of all appearances of a relaxed man who cared nothing about the outcome of their discussion, she could feel an undercurrent between them. A clash of wills.

There were moments he flirted and set her heart racing. Other times, like now, he seemed remote. She couldn't gauge her effect on him and it disturbed her because she was accustomed to red-blooded thirtysomething males succumbing to her charms or trying to charm her. Especially when she had flirted with them.

"Do you own the red limo?" he asked.

"No, I leased it for this trip. We flew to Dallas and picked it up there."

"You always travel with this staff?"

She shook her head. "No. My assistant, Amy, works for me full-time since the success of my first book. Virginia Boyden, a camera operator—she's a field operator who works for the show and her husband, Duke Boyden, is my chauffeur, whom I've known forever. He worked for my mom, so he's like a relative. He drives for others, too. I hire him when I need him. I don't travel like this as much for the show as for background for my next book."

"Busy person, accustomed to getting what you want."

"I think that description fits you best. You're the oldest of your siblings, aren't you?" she asked.

"Yes, just the same as you are."

"So tell me about your life, Sheriff Milan. Why are you sheriff? You don't have to do that if you don't want to."

"My family has an old tradition. All the Milan males go into law—enforcing the law, practicing law, creating laws. For the most part in our family all Milan males get a law degree and practice law, which I did for three years, but, like my brother Tony, I'm a rancher at heart, so since I can afford to do what I want, ranching is what I've done most of the time. People in town wanted me to run for sheriff in the last election and I let them talk me into it."

"So I heard. According to gossip, people trust you and they think you're an honest man. When the Wrenville house reverts fully to the town of Verity and a fortune is found hidden away in the house, you're the man people will trust. That's a high recommendation about you."

"I was honored and it was something I could do to contribute to my town," he said.

She believed him. In spite of their clash, she was not only physically attracted to him, but she was also beginning to like him. She could see why people in town liked him.

"So what do all your brothers do?"

"Nick is a state representative. His background is the law firm of Milan, Thornridge and Appleton. Tony has a law degree, went to work for the firm for a year and then quit to be a rancher, his first love. We all love our ranches. My sister, Madison, is an artist and a newlywed."

"Madison Milan Calhoun—a very successful and very talented artist. I stopped in her gallery here. Am I allowed to write about this family tradition of male Milans going into law?"

"If you want."

"It'll add to my story about the Milans."

"Frankly, I hope you decide to not have any story about the Milans, the Calhouns or Verity," he said. "We're really a small, quiet town. Or we were until today."

She just smiled at him.

The limo parked in front of the entrance to the three-story, Tudor-style country club in Dallas. Soft music played and a fountain splashed as they walked inside. Destiny was conscious of being close at Wyatt's side, even more aware of him following her across the restaurant, her back tingling because she was certain his gaze was on her. After they entered a small private room, the waiter took orders for their drinks and left.

As soon as they were alone, she smiled across the linen-covered table at Wyatt. "A private room with music from the large dining room, flowers, candlelight—you've taken care of everything."

"Not quite everything yet," he said in a tone that was as disturbing as his touch. "Sorry if you hoped to give another interview to the local press."

She didn't ask what he hadn't taken care of, having a feeling it involved her. "No. This is much nicer. Now I can hear more about the history and people of Verity and the Milans," she said, but her thoughts were on Wyatt, curious about him. "So tell me about your family."

"We're an ordinary family. My dad is a judge and he lives here in Dallas with my mom. I told you earlier that I have two brothers and one sister who live close to me. That's my family. If I remember correctly about yours, your mom was an actress and your father was a scriptwriter and later a director and now both are deceased. You're a Californian and you grew up in L.A. You've never been married. You have a background in television and cohosted a California show about celebrities. Now you host your own successful show from Chicago, *Unsolved Mysteries,* which has done well. You're also a published author."

"You're correct so far. Good memory," she said.

He stood and came around to take her hand. "Care to dance? I saw couples dancing when we came in."

Smiling at him, she placed her hand in his, experiencing a tingle from the physical contact. When they reached the dance floor, she was happy the band played rock with an enthusiastic small crowd on the floor. He dropped her hand as they began to dance. She was surprised how well

he danced, reminding herself not to underestimate him.
She danced around him, aware of his blue eyes constantly
on her, a dance that was exhilarating and fun, allowing
her to release pent-up energy.

By the third song, he caught her hand and pulled her to
the edge of the dance floor. "Let's go back and I'll shed
this coat and we can see if our drinks are here."

She nodded as the crowd sang to a familiar song while
they danced.

In their private room, Wyatt draped his jacket over a
chair. They had a wine bottle chilling and tall glasses of
ice water on the table. Wyatt drank half the glass before
he asked, "Want to dance again?"

"I'd love to. I'm surprised it's not sentimental ballads.
It sounds like a bar out there, not a country club dining
room."

"It's just people having fun."

"So what do you call fun, Wyatt?"

"Dancing, laughter, friends," he said as they approached
the dance floor. At the edge of the dance floor he leaned
close to talk softly, his breath warm on her ear. "Sexy, hot
kisses, flirting with a beautiful woman." Before she could
answer him, he began to dance and she joined him, moving her body in time to the beat while she smiled at him.

He flirted and he responded to her, a reaction she often
had from men, but she hadn't expected to be drawn to him.
She was accustomed to men flirting with her, coming on
to her, but she rarely felt an intense physical response to
any of them. She never carried it further than flirting, unlike Desirée who had far too many affairs and who liked
men indiscriminately, according to Destiny's thinking.

Destiny's gaze rested on Wyatt's mouth and she wondered what it'd be like to kiss him. But hadn't she heard
that Wyatt had part of himself locked away and only one
woman had ever really touched his heart? Rumor had it that

his heart had been broken when his fiancée had returned his ring and he'd never had another serious relationship.

She barely knew Wyatt, but once or twice she had seen a shuttered look in his eyes and felt he had closed himself off emotionally. Physically, he made it obvious that he desired her, but nothing beyond that. Far from it, since she no doubt annoyed him with her purpose in coming to Verity.

She couldn't understand her reaction to him. She couldn't control her racing pulse or breathlessness or the tingles dancing over her insides. Wyatt was handsome but he wasn't her type. He was a laid-back, quiet, cowboy sheriff, a cowboy who loved his ranch, a man accustomed to running things and getting his way. How could she find him exciting?

The men she enjoyed in Chicago and in L.A. were more outgoing, enjoyed the theater, concerts, art exhibits. Some had been involved in television—men more like her. She and Wyatt were poles apart in backgrounds, personalities, ambitions, likes and dislikes. The only reason they were out tonight was because he wanted to talk her out of filming the Wrenville house and because he had promised to tell her the history about the killings in the house. This wasn't a regular date. Even though they flirted, laughed and danced, she could feel the constant clash of wills. And he was going to be even more annoyed with her soon, when she announced she was a Calhoun descendant. A faint chill made her shiver while she had a premonition of the bad moments to come. It would be one more clash between them, perhaps one bad enough to end any friendliness beginning to develop between them.

Throwing herself into the dance, she blocked out thoughts about the Calhouns and the Milans and just enjoyed being with an appealing, sexy man, the anticipation of finding some answers to old secrets of the town of Verity and, most of all, finding material for an intriguing show.

She had no intention of leaving Verity without doing what she had come to do. She was more interested now in the unsolved murders than she had been before.

As they danced, Wyatt's blue eyes were on her every move. Occasionally they brushed against each other. Would he kiss her good-night? The errant thought pulled her up short. When had she wondered that on a first date before? Probably not since she had been sixteen years old. But she was almost certain he would kiss her. He had seemed on the verge of it almost half a dozen times since he had walked into his office to meet her. And this wasn't a date, she reminded herself. The whole evening was meant to discourage her as far as the sheriff was concerned. So why, she asked herself, was he such good company?

When they finally returned to their table, Wyatt pulled on his jacket again.

"You don't need to wear your jacket. We're in a private room and I don't mind."

"I'm with a beautiful Chicago television personality who has her own show—I think I'll wear my jacket," he said.

"Thank you."

They both became silent when the waiter entered the room with their salads.

"I'm not talking you out of filming and investigating the Wrenville house, am I?" Wyatt asked as they began to eat. "Or of forgetting about the family feud?"

"Not at all. I'm not going to be in the Wrenville house forever—just briefly. It's a big house. You can come join us and watch if you want."

"No thanks. I'm not appearing on a TV show."

"We might make a deal—you give me an interview about being a Milan, about the Wrenville house and what you think you'll find there next year and you can name what you want in return."

"Cut Verity totally and I'll give you the interview," he countered.

"If I don't film the Wrenville house, then the interview will be useless," she replied.

"Your camera operator is with you to film or to take pictures of the house?"

"To take pictures. We're just in the earliest stages right now. I want to find out if there is enough material for a show and if it's interesting, things like that. This is preliminary to take back and present as a possible show."

"Isn't it unusual for the host to be doing all this investigation?" Wyatt asked.

"Yes, but I'm deeply involved with the show and I've come up with some other stories that were produced. Also, this is important information for my next book."

"Sounds as if the book is the major reason."

"It is an intriguing story if I can find enough information about it. There must be old newspapers on file about the murders. I have an appointment tomorrow with the head of the Library Board and I'm going to the Verity genealogy society office."

"What I've told you will be repeated in the paper. Beyond what I've said, I don't think there's much more about it."

"We'll see what I can find."

"Do I need to come out with you and check there is no vagrant living there now?"

Smiling, she shook her head. "No. My chauffeur will be with us. Duke is a retired police officer who is a chauffeur now."

"Ah, an ex-cop. That's the first good news since I saw your red limo in my parking place."

She laughed and leaned forward, placing her hand on his forearm, feeling the solid muscle through his sleeves. "The first good news? I'm disappointed. You rate that above meeting me, above this evening together, above dancing with me—"

He leaned over the table until his face was inches from hers and she felt as if she was drowning in his blue eyes. "You're out with me, dancing with me, because you want something from me. Not one second of this evening is because you want to be spending the evening with me."

His words were harsh, but the look in his eyes wasn't. His gaze conveyed desire and she couldn't move or catch her breath. Her heart pounded. If the table hadn't been between them, she would have expected him to kiss her right there and she wanted him to, which shocked her.

"That isn't exactly accurate," she said breathlessly. "You felt something when we met—deny that, Wyatt."

"Okay, so I did. You're a beautiful, sexy woman."

The words heated her and her desire intensified. "I wanted to go out with you tonight and I think you've enjoyed this evening, too," she whispered.

"I have, but I can't forget that you want something from me."

"That doesn't have one thing to do with having fun dancing with you," she said, still breathless. "We—"

She stopped and sat back as they heard a slight knock on the door right before it opened. Their waiter brought their dinners—prime rib for Wyatt and chicken breast for her.

While they ate, Wyatt told her about Texas legends he knew and she tried to charm him, realizing she was having a better time than she had had in a long time. After dinner they danced to more loud rock and it wasn't until over an hour later when the band played a ballad that Wyatt took her in his arms to slow dance.

Being in his arms heightened her awareness of him, made her think of kisses and wanting to be alone with him. She danced with him, aware of his height, his body against hers, his legs brushing hers.

"I think you've been scared to slow-dance with me. It's taken until almost midnight for us to have this first slow dance," she teased.

He looked down at her and she couldn't get her breath. "Fear isn't the emotion I've experienced with you," he said. His voice had lowered again, that warm, husky timbre that was as tangible as a caress. "Far from it. You know the effect you have. I want you in my arms, Destiny. I have all night."

Her heart began to thud and as they pressed lightly together while they danced, she wondered if he could feel her heartbeats.

"You want me, Wyatt, even though I don't think you like me."

"Like? You're spectacular, a gorgeous woman. I've enjoyed being with you tonight." A muscle worked in his jaw and his eyes were a vivid blue.

"Thank you, but I don't believe you're really dazzled. Maybe I've started something here that I shouldn't have," she whispered.

"You started it when you entered my office today," he said. "As they say, 'Be careful what you wish for.'"

"That applies to you, too."

He spun her around and dipped her low so she had to cling to him as she gazed into blue eyes that conveyed his desire. She forgot the other dancers, the band, everything except Wyatt. He made her want to close her eyes and raise her lips to his for a kiss. He swung her up and they stood on the dance floor for an instant while her heart drummed and she couldn't move. Then he began to dance again, dancing her to the sidelines.

"Ready to head home?" he asked in a voice that implied much more.

"Yes," she answered. He took her arm lightly to walk

back to their table, leaving the door open as they entered the small room and she retrieved her purse.

In the limo ride back to the airport, and in the plane, she couldn't take her eyes off him. Her whole body seemed to vibrate with the anticipation of what was to come when they touched down in Verity.

Finally, when they reached her hotel and he helped her out of the car, she turned to him. "Would you like to come up for a drink, Wyatt?" she asked.

"I'd like that," he replied, following her to her suite.

She could feel him watching her, and her back tingled as she walked ahead of him into the living area. "You've probably been in these suites before, haven't you?"

He nodded. "The old-fashioned furniture was selected to replicate the early-day furnishings of the hotel."

She watched while he dropped his suit jacket on a chair and loosened his tie to unbutton the collar button. His gaze held hers and there was no mistaking the desire she saw in his eyes.

"There's a fully stocked bar," she said. "What would you like to have?"

He closed the distance between them, standing in front of her, and she couldn't get her breath as she looked up at him. While her heart hammered, she anticipated his kiss.

"Finally," he said softly, sliding his arm around her waist and pulling her up tightly against him in a way he had not done while they had been dancing.

Her insides twisted and heated, her breasts tingling as his gaze lowered slowly and he looked down at her.

"I've been waiting all night for this." One by one he drew the pins out of her hair until finally her red locks spilled over her shoulders and fell in disarray around her face.

With both hands he combed his fingers through the curly locks, and the light tugs on her scalp were tantalizing. Desire was intense, a yearning she couldn't understand because she'd never felt it so strongly, and for Wyatt, of all people, someone who was blocking what she wanted. They were at odds, no matter how civil they both were. Unlike her grandmother she couldn't blame it on Wyatt being a Milan while she was a Calhoun. This wasn't because of a feud. It was because they were at cross-purposes. His goal was to keep the status quo of his quiet life and town while hers was to unravel the mysteries of the past that might undo Wyatt's peace at the same time.

She was afraid he would find a way to keep her out of the house or keep her from airing the show later. Yet at the moment, none of that mattered. All she knew now was that his arms were around her and she was caught and held in the compelling vivid blue of his thickly lashed eyes. She turned her face up slightly. Stubborn sheriff, a Milan—it no longer mattered. She wanted his kiss.

All the time he had freed her hair, he had gazed into her eyes, the depths of his conveying a promise of pleasure.

Wanting him with an intensity that had built through the evening, she tilted her head, closing her eyes to relish the feel of his hard body against hers, his arms holding her tightly. Finally his mouth covered hers. With her heart pounding, she wrapped her arms around his neck, clinging tightly, feeling her world shift and change. His kiss was possessive, as if he were taking her heart, claiming her as his own. She trembled with sudden hunger and need.

She savored being in his embrace and kissing him, feeling his rock-solid muscles pressed against her, his arms holding her tightly while his kisses made her want to be free of the barriers between them.

"Wyatt," she whispered, feeling the stubble of his beard against her lips, running her fingers in his thick hair at the back of his head.

"Wyatt," she repeated, pulling his head close again and

pressing her mouth against his, her tongue tangling with his. All evening Wyatt had teased, flirted, touched and danced and all her pent-up control had spilled out. Now desire became a white-hot flame that consumed her. It had been a long, long time since a man had made love to her.

She never felt Wyatt's fingers undoing the buttons on the sleeve and shoulder of her dress, but after the kiss, he leaned away a fraction and lowered the top part of her dress. Cool air brushed her shoulders, and her heart drummed as he looked at her and cupped her breasts, his thumbs playing lightly over the sensitive buds, making her gasp.

She had come to Verity for research, and had given little thought to meeting Wyatt. She had never expected to be swept off her feet this way. She hadn't expected to feel this dizzying need for his kisses and caresses, or the hungry longing that she hadn't experienced before. Her reaction to him, both physical and emotional, shocked her each time they had touched, but now in his arms with him kissing her senseless, kisses that claimed possession, that threatened to capture her heart, her need for him consumed her. She gasped for breath, raising her head slightly to look at him, and the impact of the need in his expression made her knees go weak and heightened what she felt. Her fingers went to his shirt and she opened the buttons until she pushed his shirt away.

She ran her fingers over his rock-hard, sculpted chest. Locks of dark hair had fallen on his forehead and his mouth was red from their kisses. She closed her eyes as desire rocked her while he caressed her breasts lightly.

"You're beautiful," he whispered, burying his face against her softness, his tongue stroking her.

With a moan of pleasure, she ran her fingers through his thick, coarse hair. Sliding her hand down over his broad shoulder, she felt the solid muscles. As he suckled her breast, she gasped.

He raised his head and looked down at her with hooded eyes. Drawing her to him, he leaned over her, kissing her possessively until she was on fire and all reason had fled.

She clung to him, dimly aware this was what she had wanted, yet feeling she was the one headed for heartbreak and Wyatt was the one taking her heart. She didn't want to feel this desperate need for him and for his loving. She didn't want to lose her control.

"Wyatt, wait," she said, leaning away and gasping for breath at the same time as she wanted to pull him back and remove the last barriers of clothing between them. "We just met—"

"I don't think that matters," he whispered. "You want this. You made that clear with our first kiss." He drew her into his embrace again. His gaze devoured her, his hands stroked her and he pushed her dress over her hips, letting it fall around her ankles.

She moaned. Lost in a haze of desire, she couldn't think straight. A part of her knew this was where the evening was headed as she flirted with him, but was lovemaking what she had really intended? She couldn't answer that question, as his kiss demolished all thought and she could do nothing but yield to the passion he incited in her.

She showered her own kisses on him, trailing them down across his chest, running her fingers over his hard muscles. He groaned and pulled her up to kiss her.

With clothing soon tossed aside, Wyatt picked her up and carried her to bed.

His hands drifted over her in light, feathery caresses that built her need to a fever pitch. Finally, one thought broke through.

"Wyatt, I don't have protection."

His eyes narrowed a fraction before he left to get a

packet from his wallet. When he returned, she caressed his thighs, wanting him more than she would have ever dreamed possible. How could she want this man who was so totally different from everything in her life? How could she feel this way about him when she had just met him hours earlier? She ached to pull him close, to make love and hold him. She knew he had no idea how rare, how shocking her reaction to him was.

He came down to kiss her, sliding his arm beneath her to hold her to him, and as he entered her slowly, he paused. It had been a long time since she had made love and she suspected he had been startled, but the hesitation was fleeting and gone as she tightened her arms to hold him.

With a cry she arched to meet him, and when she had taken him fully she moved with him, in perfect synchronization, as if they had known each other's bodies for years.

She sensed that he struggled for control, felt the sweat beading on his shoulders and brow. Yet he continued kissing her, pumping and filling her, and he drove her to the brink.

"Wyatt," she cried his name, torn from her in a pounding need for his loving as her long legs tightened around him. She held him against her heart, moving with him, dazed and spinning into ecstasy.

Release burst with a fury, a blinding surge of fulfillment and rapture that spilled over her. With one last thrust he groaned and climaxed, taking her with him to another heart-stopping release. She gasped for breath as she clung to him, lost in sensation.

As their pulse returned to normal, his weight came down on her and she ran her fingers over him and hugged him against her heart. Lost in euphoria, she would have to sort out her thoughts and feelings later.

Wyatt rolled on his side, taking her with him while they clung to each other. She was conscious of one emotion. Shock. She was shocked by how desperately she had wanted him, how strongly she felt for him. Right now she didn't ever want to leave his arms.

"You're a sexy, beautiful woman, Destiny," he whispered, kissing her temple, then trailing tender little kisses to her mouth. "I think we might have been headed to this moment since we met," he said.

Smiling at him, she raised slightly to place her mouth on his, her tongue stroking his, stirring his arousal.

He pulled her down to kiss her hungrily, hard and passionately, as if they hadn't just made love. In minutes, he rolled over her, moving between her legs.

Her heartbeat raced as the fire he'd sparked in her ignited into flame. She wanted him more than ever and more than she would have thought possible. She felt bereft when he moved from her to get protection and then rejoiced when he drew her into his embrace once again.

All logic and thought had stopped and she moved blindly, yielding to desire, not weighing consequences.

Pulling her to sit astride him, he entered her. They moved in unison, a heart-pounding rhythm that sent her into a dizzying spiral of need. His hands roamed over her, storming her senses until she cried out in ecstasy along with him.

She fell across him, holding him, while he wrapped an arm around her waist and kissed her.

He looked at her, brushing locks of curly hair away from her face. "You're an enigma."

"You could tell I haven't made love in a long, long time. There haven't been many men in my whole life that I've been deeply involved with," she said, wondering whether that scared him or not. "News you may find difficult to believe. I know I convey a different image."

"That you do. You surprise me again. You've been a steady stream of surprises," he said, running his fingers lightly over her lower lip. She brushed a kiss on his hand and he smiled at her.

"You're casting your own spell, Destiny."

"You're incredibly sexy, but even so, I'm not going to agree to pack and go home because you want me to."

"I don't recall asking or giving you any conditions before we made love," he said, toying with her hair as he talked.

He turned on his side and held her close so she lay facing him. "You're stunning."

She felt a blush heat her cheeks. "On one level we can communicate and we're compatible, thank goodness. For a while our differences became minimized. When you see that I'm not going to cause the town harm, maybe we can get along."

"I'd say we're getting along rather well," he said, toying with her bare breasts and stirring her yearnings again.

"Yes, we are, Wyatt," she whispered. She raked her fingers slowly through his hair, watching the short, dark brown strands spring back. "I want you to stay here in my arms tonight. It's already more than half past two."

"Shortly, I will get up, shower and dress to go home. I don't care to have it all over town tomorrow that we were together here all night."

She smiled and traced circles on his bare chest and ripped abdomen. "You're embarrassed for people to know you're with me?"

"Of course not. I'm a private person and like to keep what I do private if possible. I suspect you don't understand that and you don't feel that way. You're a public figure and it's good for your career to have the world want to know about you." He shrugged. "To each his own."

She laughed. "I'm accustomed to attention and I'm not sure with my bright auburn hair I could keep people from noticing me even if I wanted to."

"Beautiful hair. I like your hair," he said, playing with the long strands and letting them curl around his fingers. They looked into each other's eyes and once again she felt that sizzling current of electricity arc in the air between them to send sparks flying.

Breaking the circuit, he stood up and grabbed his suit pants. "I'll shower and dress and go."

"So we're not going to see each other again?" she asked, pulling the sheet to her chin and placing her hands behind her head. The sheet followed the curves of her body.

He leaned down, sliding an arm beneath her and kissing her. His mouth was hard, possessive, his tongue stroking hers slowly.

Moaning softly she wrapped her arms around his neck to return his kiss. He raised his head a fraction. "We'll see each other again and we'll make love again. This hot attraction hasn't cooled yet for either one of us. I can feel your pulse and it's racing as much as mine is," he said in a husky voice.

Releasing her, he walked away, gathering the rest of his clothes and then leaving the room without looking back.

She got up to pick up her things and go to the shower in her adjoining bathroom, still tingling and wanting Wyatt's kisses, his touch and his body in bed next to hers for the rest of the night. How had it never occurred to her how much she wanted him, or that she would respond to him the way she had? It was a surprise development and one she didn't want or like. They were very different people with a feud and an old house between them. The Wrenville project and the feud could become bigger problems in their lives, something Wyatt had already made clear he didn't want to happen. Even so, she couldn't stop wanting him. Her desires and responses were not going away and she wouldn't be able to ignore them. Was she in any danger of falling in love with him?

She dismissed the thought as ridiculous. She had never been deeply, truly in love in her whole life. The sheriff of Verity, Texas, was certainly not going to capture her heart. Even though he was a billionaire, successful and sexy beyond any other man she had ever known, he was a rancher, a cowboy, a sheriff and a West Texan, as remote from her world as the moon from earth.

She was astounded that she had liked making love and being out with him. She paused to think about the past evening. She'd had the best time ever, made love with the sexiest man ever. It had been a night she would never forget, even though she wanted to. She didn't want this heart-pounding, breathtaking reaction. This rancher was not the man to fit into her life and she needed to get over this intense response to him.

She half expected making love would shoo away the pesky attraction, but it hadn't. At least, not yet. She wanted to get him back into the proper perspective—that of an ordinary man, like all others in town. Then, when she left Verity, she'd simply forget Wyatt.

She showered, dressed in jeans and a sweatshirt, and followed the aroma of freshly brewed coffee into the kitchen.

He was seated at the kitchen table, sipping a cup of coffee. When she entered, he came to his feet, his gaze drifting over her. Tall, lanky, moving with a lazy ease that hid the strength he had, he set her heart pounding despite her resolve. "I thought I'd have a little fortification before I head home," he said. "Can I pour you a cup?"

"I'll get it, thank you. Sit again and I'll join you." She poured a cup and carried it to the table. He stood waiting, holding out her chair, and as she walked up, they gazed at each other. Once again, she was held by his blue eyes that conveyed so much heat, it was difficult to catch her breath.

Without looking at it, he took her coffee and set it down

with one hand. He slipped his other hand across her nape and drew her close to kiss her. All her intentions to view him the way she did other men dissolved and vanished.

While she returned his kiss, his arms banded her waist. Shoving the chair away, he drew her fully against him and it was as if they hadn't made love only a short time earlier.

When he finally released her, both of them were breathing hard. "I'm not staying the rest of the night," he said, more as if to remind himself than to inform her.

She sat at the table, her coffee in front of her.

"You've been a surprise in nearly every way," she said, looking intently at him.

"I have to say that you have, too. You're not at all like your sister."

"No, we're not alike, but we've always been close. Mom was sick from the time Desirée was little until we lost her when Desirée was seventeen, so in some ways I guess I've been a mother to her all her life. Our mom was a model, then later she was involved in advertising and always busy. I took care of Desirée." She couldn't count the times she'd been there for her sister, willingly, patiently. "I'm the one who gives the impression of liking men, but that's really Desirée. I've been intimate with very few—I can count them on one hand easily. My sister? She could count them on one hand in high school. She collects men like some women collect jewelry. I've talked to her about her lifestyle, but she's headstrong and there are parts of her life I can't influence."

"At least you tried. A sister can't do anything else. I'd hate to try to change my sister."

"Ah, being stubborn runs in the family," she said lightly and he chuckled.

"Takes two to have 'stubborn.'" Finishing his coffee, he set the cup in the saucer, carried it to the sink to rinse and placed it in the dishwasher. "I'll go now, Destiny."

She followed him to the door of her suite, her gaze running from his thick, dark brown hair, down across broad shoulders to his narrow waistline and then down his long legs. He carried his jacket and tie on his arm.

"Thanks for telling me about the Wrenvilles," she said. "And thanks for the dinner. The evening has been great, Wyatt,"

"It has," he replied. His voice had lowered and his eyes darkened, making her draw a deep breath. "Go out again with me tonight."

"I can't, but thank you. I have a dinner date. Your mayor and his wife have invited me to their house. I couldn't refuse after such a nice letter."

"Maybe I'll see you later today," Wyatt said. They gazed at each other and she wanted him to kiss her again.

Instead of leaving, he stood there and her heart began to drum. She placed a hand lightly on his forearm. "Wyatt," she whispered, wanting his kiss, wanting him to stay.

"See you later," he said as he turned and left.

As soon as the elevator doors closed behind him, she stepped inside and locked her door. She wanted to see him again, go out with him again, even though they were at cross-purposes. With their lifestyles and careers, there was no future in any relationship between them. She had a busy life in Chicago, family in L.A. and this Wrenville project, plus her Calhoun heritage. All things Wyatt wanted no part of and would not be compatible with him. Plus, he had never opened himself up to her. She had already been warned that Wyatt kept part of himself shut away, so she didn't want to get into a relationship that would be any risk to her own heart. And Wyatt would be a heartbreaker.

What would happen when he learned she was a Calhoun? Destiny wondered whether he would even speak to her. No matter what he'd said, that old feud had not died yet or Wyatt wouldn't be so disturbed by it.

Destiny planned to be gone in a few days. It shouldn't take long to draw some conclusions about the murders. She wanted to check out old papers. Talk to locals. She wanted to find the oldest generation, talk to some of them and get their account of the story. She would be gone and soon Wyatt Milan would be forgotten.

She went back to her bedroom, eyeing the empty bed, the covers awry, seeing Wyatt there with the sheet across his middle, his lean, muscled body sexy, irresistible to her. She might not feel as if she was in danger of falling in love with him, but he was the sexiest man she'd ever met and one of only two she had really been attracted to. But what she felt for Wyatt was more intense. Maybe it was because she was older now. But at twenty-nine she still couldn't fully understand her own reactions.

She planned to make her announcement this afternoon about her Calhoun heritage. Would that end the relationship with Wyatt? A pang chilled her. Or should she keep her heritage secret? Instantly, she shook her head even though she was alone. If she did a show on the Wrenville house, some way her bloodline and her Calhoun ancestors would come out. This was the time to get the most drama out of revealing her ties to Verity and the feud before someone else broke the news. She just hoped it didn't make a world of difference to Wyatt.

She changed to cotton pajamas—not what she would have worn with Wyatt, yet what she found comfortable. As she slid into bed she could feel Wyatt's presence there, smell his scent. She thought about the evening, still surprised at how she had reacted to him and the effect he had on her. Had the evening meant anything to him?

She didn't really know him well enough to discern what he felt. So many times men she had dated and never been intimate with had claimed to be in love with her. She'd never reciprocated those emotions. In fact, she had never really been in love. Yet she had known clearly how the men felt, and when they wanted to be intimate, some of the men had proposed. It was different with Wyatt. They'd been physically intimate and yet he remained a mystery, as closed off and as much a stranger in some ways as he was when he had first walked into his office to meet her. She couldn't fathom her own feelings because she was in new territory with Wyatt. Her dealings with him in one day were light-years from those with any other man she had ever known.

One refreshing thing with Wyatt—he wasn't impressed by her fame, her television show, any of that. He seemed to be truly interested in *her* and honest with her. She didn't need to turn on the charm with him because she felt she had his full attention all the time she was with him. And he had some rare qualities that she liked—easygoing, loyal to his family and evidently close with his siblings, straightforward with her, obviously the town trusted him. He was a leader, a take-charge person, which she liked even though in her own situation, she would have been better off if he had given in to whatever she wanted.

How had she gotten so involved with him almost instantly? Her actions went against all her beliefs and all the advice she'd given to her sister over the years. One thing she knew—Wyatt was going to be difficult to forget. What was worse, he might be difficult to deal with in the coming days. She hoped he would not interfere enough to wreck her intention to have the Wrenville unsolved murders on her show. She had her own plans regarding the Milans and the Calhouns and Wyatt was not going to like what she intended to do. He wasn't going to like it at all.

Four

To his dismay, Wyatt could not shake Destiny out of his thoughts. He had slept only a few hours and then stirred, wanting her beside him. He had yearned to seduce her from the first moment he saw her and though she didn't disappoint him, she had shocked him.

Destiny conveyed hot sex. Everything about her appeared wanton, steamy and earthy, from her riot of red hair down to her long, shapely legs. Yet she'd told him she had been intimate with only a few men, and no one in the past several years.

Her sister, however, looked virginal with her Dresden Doll beauty, yet Desirée was the one who liked men and went from one relationship to another.

Yes, Destiny had surprised him. He wondered if she had ever been in love and decided to ask her the next time he had a chance.

He thought of Katherine, the woman he had thought was the love of his life. Tall, blonde, blue-eyed, she was the most beautiful woman he had known and he had loved her with his whole heart, opening himself in every way, planning a lifetime with her, expecting them to be wrapped in their love that he thought she felt as deeply as he.

It still hurt to think about the pain of their breakup. He should have seen it coming when she began to find excuses for not seeing him, but, as the saying went, love was blind. When she finally had broken it off, it had been crushing. Eventually he had gotten over Katherine, but since then he tried to keep that emotional part of his life shut away and out of his thoughts. He didn't want to risk his heart again, make himself vulnerable, get hurt like that again. He thought of his brother Nick who suffered deeply from losing his wife. Like Nick, Wyatt had no intention of giving his heart again—at least not for a long time. Hot, satisfying sex was fulfilling, but falling in love was too big a risk.

There was no risk to his heart with Destiny. She was desirable and sexy, and they'd enjoyed each other in bed, but they each could walk away without emotional damage. Their lives were vastly different and they were each accustomed to getting what they wanted so there was no danger of falling in love.

If he couldn't talk her out of it, Destiny would check out the Wrenville place and story, pack and go out of his life, and neither one of them would look back.

In the meantime, sex with her had been fantastic. Last night had been all he had hoped and then some. She was the sexiest woman he had ever known. Just thinking about her made him hot. He wished he could have stayed the rest of the night and made love again this morning but if he had been seen leaving her suite early this morning that would have stirred a firestorm of gossip and questions, including from his own family. He didn't need that drama in his life.

Then why couldn't he stop thinking about her? Destiny was a walking, talking, gorgeous threat to his peace of mind. In spite of all logic, he wanted her with him in his bed, in his arms right now.

He needed to back off. She was too unpredictable; he couldn't figure her out, which was unusual. Most people never surprised him. He didn't want Destiny falling in love with him. Her sister had been enough worry when she wanted him to go back to California with her.

He had to laugh at himself. Destiny fall in love with him? She was very much her own person, highly at odds with him over the Wrenville murders and her show. He couldn't imagine her in his life all the time. From the moment she rode into town in her big red limo, she had done nothing except stir people up. He had found a tranquil life on his ranch and in Verity and after the pain from his breakup with Katherine, he wanted peace and quiet. He guessed Destiny hadn't had peace and quiet in her life since she was five years old. She thrived on attention.

There was no way either of them would fall in love with the other. Destiny may have already moved on and shoved last night out of her mind.

Remembering the night, he paused, standing still, lost in memories. He didn't know how long he stood there, but he finally realized time had passed and he was still lost in thoughts of Destiny. He had to get to the office and he was going to be late if he didn't get moving.

Swearing under his breath, Wyatt hurried to get down a fast breakfast of cereal and leave for work.

He wanted to keep up with what Destiny would do at the Wrenville house. Writing the governor had been a smart move on her part because Wyatt couldn't overrule the governor. If it had just been the mayor, Wyatt could have seen to it that she wasn't legally allowed on the property. He'd finally gotten in touch with the governor's office to confirm Destiny's letter. She had the right to look at the old house, search it, take pictures and there was nothing he could do.

She also was free to search for a letter and a fortune or anything else she might find, but the property still belonged officially to Verity and so would anything she found.

How he wished he could legally keep her off the property, but that wasn't going to happen. She had outmaneuvered him with the governor's permission and he had to give her grudging admiration for it.

At the office he entered to find Dwight filing papers. Dwight ran his fingers through his tangled hair. "Morning. We've been getting calls. I sent them to the mayor's office. People want to know if Destiny is going to film the Wrenville house today. They want to know if she'll talk to reporters again today. The hotel called and said their lobby is filled with people waiting to get her autograph."

"Oh, hell," Wyatt said. "She'll be gone soon. Just keep telling them we don't know what she's doing or when she's doing it."

"That's what I've been saying. Mabel Lake called and wanted to know since you took Destiny out last night if you're dating. I told her that was a business evening."

"Thanks for that one and it was a business evening," he said, thinking it partially had been. "As much as any man who takes her out is going to spend a purely business evening. With her, that isn't possible."

"I don't imagine so," Dwight said wistfully. "Do you think she'll come here today?"

"I don't know what that woman is doing," Wyatt said, causing Dwight's eyes to widen. "I don't have any control over her. She has a letter from the governor of Texas giving her a big welcome and an invitation to put the Wrenville murders on her show. There's nothing I can do about it."

"Mercy. How did she get a letter from the governor?"

"She wrote him, Dwight," Wyatt replied, thinking most men would do whatever Destiny asked. Her show was popular and he imagined the governor had watched her show and knew what she looked like.

The phone rang and Dwight answered, his face wreathed in a smile until he glanced at Wyatt and his smile vanished.

"I'm fine," he said. "He's right here and headed toward his office, Ms. Jones. I'll transfer your call."

Wyatt hurried to his office and picked up his phone. "Good morning," he drawled in a deep voice.

"Morning, Wyatt," she said in a honeyed tone that made him think of last night and wish he was with her.

"I wanted to let you know we're going to the Wrenville house to look it over for the show."

"You're sure this will be a show?"

"No, not at all yet. I'll have to get everything ready and present it. I thought perhaps you'd like to drive out and see what we're doing, maybe show me where the men were murdered."

Wyatt wanted to refuse to do anything to promote the Wrenville house. On the other hand, he wanted to see Destiny. "I'll drive out later today," he said as if the words came without thought.

"Good. I have a few questions for you. We'll see you later, Wyatt. I should run now," she said. "Bye."

She was gone. Longing struck him. He wanted to see her, hold her and kiss her. He glanced at his calendar and saw calls and meetings listed. He phoned Dwight and asked him to move the 1:00 p.m. meeting. As he stared at the paperwork on his desk, he realized Destiny was already disrupting his life, just as he had feared. How much worse would it get?

It was one o'clock before he told Dwight he was leaving. After a short drive out of the east side of town, he turned into the Wrenville house. The long drive from the highway to the house was overgrown with weeds that were tamped down from recent activity. He pulled up in the drive that circled in front of the house and stopped.

He hadn't been at the place in years, had only driven by on the highway. The house was in worse shape than he had remembered. Paint was gone, the boards gray and weathered. One step had fallen in leading up to the porch, but it had been partially repaired and he suspected it was the work of the mayor getting ready for her visit. He intended to catch Gyp and talk to him about not informing him about Destiny's visit.

Windows were broken and shutters hung awry if they still hung at all. Some lay on the porch.

Chains hung where a porch swing had once been, he assumed. Moving carefully, stairs creaking beneath his weight, he climbed the stairs to the porch and watched his step, avoiding holes as he crossed to knock on the door.

It opened instantly and he faced her chauffeur, a broad-shouldered man who probably outweighed him by forty pounds, all of it pure muscle. Shorter than Wyatt by half a foot, the man stood relaxed, yet Wyatt felt he was being studied carefully.

"Hi. I'm Sheriff Wyatt Milan," Wyatt said, extending his hand.

"Duke Boyden," the chauffeur said, giving Wyatt a firm handshake.

"Former police officer, Destiny said."

"Yes, sir. I moved to Chicago when Destiny went because my wife is with the television show."

"I came to see what's going on and if Destiny is still going ahead with plans to use this place for a show."

"She's looking around. I think she has some questions for you. Come in."

As he stepped back, Wyatt entered a wide hallway that

ran through the house. He glanced around to see the house had been cleaned. Cobwebs and dust had disappeared. While the place looked abandoned, run-down and dilapidated, it was no longer filled with leaves, debris and dust.

"Wyatt," Destiny said, her throaty voice making him think about the previous night. She came into the hall from one of the rooms and a pretty brown-haired woman followed her. "I see you met Duke. Meet Amy Osgood, my cousin. She's my assistant. Amy, this is Sheriff Wyatt Milan."

"It's just Wyatt. Glad to meet you," he said, shaking her hand, finding it difficult to shift his gaze from Destiny, whose clinging red sweater held his attention. Her tight designer jeans were snug on her tiny waist, flaring over her hips. He remembered trailing his hands over those curves last night, and desire bombarded him once again. He met her gaze, unable to look away, feeling she was thinking about the same thing.

"This place looks clean," he said after a stretch of silence. "I'm surprised."

"Thank Mayor Nash. He had a cleaning crew come. I told him if there are bloodstains, to leave them alone. I don't want evidence of the shootings cleaned away. According to one of your librarians, after the murders, the front room was closed and never used again," Destiny said.

"I wouldn't be surprised because Lavita lived here alone. She had servants and some probably lived in the house, but they wouldn't have used the formal parlor. So you've talked to Philomena Latham. She's very knowledgeable about the town and the library."

Destiny nodded. "She was interesting. I talked to her before I came to town."

Wyatt wondered how many people had known she was coming to town before he did. He tried to focus on what she was telling him.

"Too bad the furniture is gone." She glanced over her shoulder. "We're looking the house over now. We just got here about an hour ago. We started upstairs and have worked our way down to this floor."

"So you haven't seen much of this floor."

"Nothing. There are a lot of stains on these old floors so I can't go by the stains," she said, her voice a notch lower. "We've just barely covered this floor and Amy and Duke are trying to map out the place, but it's difficult and each floor is different."

"You're right. I know from staying here years ago that the house has big rooms and tiny rooms. There's a large attic and a big basement. There's a storm cellar in the back that shares a wall with the basement, but there is no way to go back and forth from the basement."

As Wyatt walked at her side, he reached around her to open doors, and he caught the scent of her perfume, a heady, heavy, sensual scent that made him wish they were alone. He followed her into a kitchen with a high ceiling and cabinets with doors missing, glass broken in some of the doors. When they entered, a slender blonde turned to face him.

"Virginia, meet Sheriff Wyatt Milan. Wyatt, this is Virginia Boyden, who is fantastic with a camera."

"Hi, Virginia," Wyatt said, shaking her small hand.

"Glad to meet you, Sheriff," she said and looked at Destiny. "I'll go to the front room—that's the important room."

As Virginia left the room, Destiny looked around. "This must be a kitchen, but it doesn't resemble one."

"Think how old this house is. The kitchen was supposed to be the latest thing when it was built with piped-in water," Wyatt replied.

"I'm glad I didn't live in that era."

As she looked around, Wyatt looked at her. He could hear the others talking in the front part of the house, their voices sounding hollow in the empty spaces. He was alone with Destiny and he was tempted to step close and kiss her, but someone could return at any time.

She turned her head, her red hair swinging across her shoulders. "Wyatt—" Whatever she had been about to say was lost as he stepped forward.

"I've thought about you all day long," he said. He held her chin lightly with his fingers. "I've remembered every moment of our night together."

"Wyatt, we're not alone. I have three people with me."

"Kisses seem more urgent and more important to me than this old house," he said, giving her another long, intense look before turning away.

He heard her take a deep breath. "Come on, Sheriff, let's look at the front parlor. The others are already in there."

Wyatt took her arm. The minute he touched her, everything faded except memories of the night with her. He wanted to be with her tonight, wanted to get her to his house where they could stay undisturbed and he wouldn't have to leave in the middle of the night. He inhaled deeply, smelling her perfume that triggered more memories. He didn't want this intense reaction to her. Destiny was an increasing disruption in his quiet life. Even as he thought that, he couldn't stop looking at her and wanting to be with her through the night. He wanted, needed to kiss her.

As if she knew what he was thinking, she glanced up at him. His insides tightened and he could feel the current between them as his gaze lowered to the enticing V of her red sweater. "I like your sweater," he said, running his finger along the neckline, down to the V, feeling her softness and aching to hold her.

She stepped away. "Wyatt—" she said, her voice breathless. She stepped past him and he caught up to walk down the hall to a large room. Some windows were broken and some boarded up, casting shadows on a stone fireplace at one end of the room.

"We could have a basketball game in this room," Duke said from behind him and Wyatt turned slightly while he glanced at the high ceilings.

"You're right. This is probably the formal parlor and as far as I know, it's where the shootings took place."

Duke strolled slowly around, looking at holes in the walls.

Wyatt glanced at the ancient and aging floor that had many stains. "Some of these are the bloodstains. I've never known exactly which ones because it's never been important to know."

Destiny stopped and looked at a large brown stain on the worn wooden floor. "I have an appointment with Philomena again later this afternoon."

"She may be helpful," he said, sorry he had not been particularly helpful about town history, but he didn't care to encourage Destiny. "What time is your appointment?"

"Not until four o'clock today," she replied. She looked around the floor again. "Amy, you stand where one bloodstain is. Duke, you stand where one is and I'm at what has to be one."

As they moved into place, she looked at Virginia. "Virginia, take pictures of us and then when we move away, get the stains in the floor so I'll have some pictures of possibly where the men stood the fatal night."

Wyatt watched her, he couldn't help thinking about her and wanting to be alone with her. He wanted to make love more than he had before last night.

Surprising him, Destiny said, "I think we might as well get back to town and let me get the information about the killings because that's what will be important. If there isn't much story or mystery here, then none of this matters. We'll pack and go and forget this project." She looked

at Wyatt. "You still have a chance of getting your way. I'll
know after I talk more to people in town about what they
know and see how much information we can get about the
night of the murders and about Lavita Wrenville."

She glanced at her staff. "Let's go back to the hotel to
regroup. I have some appointments." She walked to Wyatt
to loop her arm in his. "Unless you can tell me more about
that night or steer me to someone else I should talk to in
town, I'll have to tell you goodbye."

"Not goodbye." They stepped into the hall and he took
her arm to draw her with him into the next room, which
was a dining room. Wyatt closed the door quietly.

"Wyatt, what are you doing?"

"Giving us some privacy," he said in a husky tone as
he returned.

Her voice was shaky when she replied, "I'll call you
later tonight."

Wyatt glanced at the closed door and then back at her.
"I want you, Destiny. I want to make love to you again and
I will. And you want me, too, don't you?"

She hesitated a moment. "You know the answer to your
question," she whispered, gazing back at him intently. "But
now I should join the others." She brushed past him to
leave the room.

Did she feel the same as he did—wanting more than
anything to have another night together? Or was she having regrets? She didn't act like a woman with regrets.

When Wyatt caught up with her and her crew, everyone started to gather the equipment that was piled near the
door. Duke took some equipment from Virginia's hand and
shook his head at Amy. "You ladies go ahead to the car.
I'll bring these things."

"I can get the rest," Wyatt said easily. "We'll get it all."

As he gathered camera equipment, tablets, laptops and
notebooks, Duke worked beside him. At the front door

Duke paused, turning to face Wyatt. "My boss leaves a general impression with most men she meets," Duke said casually, looking around the room and then letting his gaze rest on Wyatt. "It usually isn't correct. Contrary to what she conveys and how she appears, there have been few men in her life."

Wyatt was startled that Duke would relay such personal information to a total stranger. He focused more closely on the man, whose brown eyes were intent on Wyatt.

"I just don't want to see her hurt," Duke said. "She's not Desirée who was mad as hell because she's accustomed to getting her way. Desirée's a kid with unreasonable expectations, immature and spoiled. Success and fame came when she was too young to handle it. Destiny tries to protect her, but of course, she can't and now Destiny is in Chicago, far away from her sister. Destiny is entirely different. I don't want to see her get hurt."

Wyatt's eyes narrowed and he tilted his head to one side. "Did you just threaten me?"

"Not at all," Duke said, smiling at Wyatt, a cold smile that Wyatt considered unfriendly. "I would never, ever threaten a sheriff. No, I'm just talking and giving you some information about Destiny so you understand the woman you're dealing with a little better. Men get the wrong impression about Destiny because of her looks, the way she dresses and she comes on friendly and smiling, usually turning on the charm. It's a front to get what she wants, to get attention. It's only a surface thing. Like I said, I just don't want her hurt."

"Don't worry where I'm concerned. I barely know her."

"When we travel, I try to look out for my wife and also Amy and Destiny. Destiny seems interested in you."

"I'd just as soon she would give this up and go on to something else. There are far more interesting unsolved mysteries in Texas. There's no need to stir up old animosities," Wyatt said. "See you, Duke." He stepped outside and deposited everything he carried behind the man's car. When he noticed Destiny waiting at his car, he walked over to her.

"Thanks for carrying out stuff," she said. "Call me."

"I'll keep in touch," he said.

"Bye, Wyatt. Thanks for coming out." She left him standing there, watching her for a moment, remembering the night and wanting her with him again.

Wyatt drove to his house in Verity that he had built when he got elected sheriff so he wouldn't have to commute daily from his ranch. In an exclusive gated community, his home was on five acres, set back with trees hiding it from the winding street. He drove around to enter in the back and as he got a cold beer, he heard his phone beep with a text from Nick and one from Tony. Both still wanted to know when they could meet Destiny.

He shook his head and thought about her. He wanted to see her again himself. He wanted to be alone with her and have a complete night with her. Or longer. Even knowing that she was nothing but trouble in the long run. He walked down the hall to the room that he used for an office. Looking at the calendar, he tried to figure when he could ask her to his place for a cookout and invite his brothers. Madison had just married Jake Calhoun and Wyatt didn't know whether they were even back yet from their honeymoon. He didn't think either one of them would have a shred of interest in meeting Destiny. He left messages for all of them and then stood staring into space, lost in thought about Destiny. He had no idea how soon she would go back to Chicago.

From the first moment in his office, she had stormed his senses and he had wanted to get to know her. He had wanted to seduce her and when he did, she had been far more than he had expected. She had left him wanting her more than ever and unable to get her out of his thoughts.

Wyatt drove back to his office, stopping to talk to people on the way and going to his desk to look at his calendar and think about when he could have her out for dinner.

He mulled over his talk with Duke—Duke who had been so protective of the women, checking out Wyatt, threatening him. In spite of his denial, it had been a threat and Duke looked like the type who meant what he said. Wyatt recalled clearly facing Duke, receiving the warning.

"My boss leaves a general impression with most men she meets.... Contrary to what she conveys and how she appears, there have been few men in her life.... I just don't want her hurt."

So now he might have to worry about Duke. How much more was Destiny going to complicate and change his life? What would she do next?

Five

Wednesday morning Duke drove Destiny down Main Street, parking behind the sheriff's car in front of city hall. He held the door for Destiny who stepped out and strolled in to ask Dwight to tell Wyatt that she would like to see him.

In seconds he appeared and her heart beat faster at the sight of him. In his freshly pressed plain brown sheriff's uniform, he took her breath away. She knew movie stars, celebrities, politicians and none of those men had the dazzling effect that Wyatt did. What was the chemistry between them and how long would it last? Wyatt was not the person she wanted to feel steaming attraction to at all. She still couldn't believe how attracted she was to him and how after making love with him, she only wanted more.

The moment she looked into Wyatt's eyes she remembered their night together. His gaze swept over her, a quick glance, yet it sped her already racing heartbeat.

"Hi," he said. "Come into my office."

"Good morning," she said breathlessly, smiling at him and walking past him.

Shedding her jacket, she sat in a leather chair opposite his. This time his gaze traveled slowly over her. "You should have stopped traffic out on Main Street in those jeans and that sweater," he said and she smiled, smoothing the low-cut V neckline of her purple sweater.

"No, I was hidden away inside the red limo and all was quiet as usual."

"You had to get out and walk into my office. You look great. They should hire you to model jeans."

"Thank you, but I'm not the model type. Skinny? I think not. That's nice of you to say. And you can look all you want." She felt his gaze trailing over her as if it was his fingers. She wanted so badly to step into his arms and kiss him.

Wyatt redirected her attention with his question. "Now that you've seen the Wrenville house, what's the verdict?"

"I'm still interested. Whether the producer will be— that's another matter. I'm interested in it for my next book. I still have people to talk to here before I move on. I'll go back to Chicago from here and then I'm going to a little town in east Texas to look into another possibility for a show. Care to join me? We could think of ways to pass the hours," she asked, smiling at him.

"I'm tempted," he replied, his voice getting a slightly husky note. "For now, how about coming to dinner Friday night at my place? I'll admit there's a particular reason for this invitation—it's my brothers wanting to meet you. They are hounding me with texts."

"I'd be delighted." She tilted her head and perused him. "Why do I think your brothers are very different from you?"

"That's not unusual. You and your sister are different," he said.

"Friday night is fine with me," she said, glancing at her watch. "I'll look forward to meeting your family."

"Good. They've wanted to meet you since you arrived."

"Tomorrow I'm going to Dallas to talk to a librarian there because they have some articles in their archives. I have some other appointments and then I'll be back late tomorrow night, so I'll be here Friday."

"Good. That will make my family happy."

"I better go now. Actually, I came here because I'm supposed to meet Ernie Grant from the Verity Chamber of Commerce. He's giving me a tour and the history of Verity. I told him I would come to his office."

"His office is in the other side of this building. I'll show you. You have a good time," he said, standing when she did. With mere inches between them she lost her breath again as she gazed into his blue eyes.

"That is the prettiest purple sweater I've ever seen," he said, slipping his fingers beneath the neckline at her collarbone and then sliding his hand down the V. His feathery touch drifted down and she tingled, wanting his hands on her, remembering his caresses.

"Wyatt," she whispered.

He closed the sliver of space between them, sliding his arm around her waist and drawing her to him while he kissed her. She wrapped her arms around his neck and kissed him in return. Her heart raced as she inhaled the scent of his tangy aftershave, felt the hardness of his body pressed against her, tasted him, reacted to his kisses. She wanted another night with him, hours of loving.

Finally, she stepped away. "Wyatt, what you do to me is a sin," she whispered.

"No, it's not. What I want to do to you is a sin. And I will again, Destiny."

"I'm going to be late," she said, gazing up at him. She stepped away, straightening her clothing.

Wyatt held the door for her and as they entered the reception area, he pointed to a hallway.

"Take that hallway and you'll see his office or you can go out and enter through the other front door."

"I'm going to say something to Duke who's in the limo, so I'll just go the front way." She smiled at Corporal Quinby. "Thanks, Dwight. You have a real nice day," she said and he smiled in return.

"Bye, Ms. Jones," Dwight said, jumping to his feet and going to hold the front door for her, something Wyatt could not recall seeing Dwight do for anyone under seventy years of age.

"Dwight, it's Destiny. Call me Destiny," she said, pausing to look into his eyes. As he grinned, his face turned red.

"Yes, ma'am," he said. "Yes, Destiny."

As the door closed behind her, he turned and looked at Wyatt. "A man could get paralyzed looking at her," he said, blinking and pushing his glasses back up on the bridge of his nose.

"I hope not," Wyatt said, looking at the door and thinking about Destiny.

"What's funny—my wife wants to meet her because she loves her book."

"Get your wife down here and introduce them. Destiny loves people." With a sigh Wyatt went back to his office to call Nick and see about dinner. He would give Jake and Madison a call in case they were back and wanted to come meet Destiny.

When he couldn't get any of the three of them, he left word on their answering machines and then sat back to send each sibling a text, but his mind was on Destiny. Her perfume still lingered and he recalled running his fingers beneath the edge of the neckline of her sweater, feeling her warm, soft skin and curves that made him hot.

Dinner at his place—and then when the brothers left, he would have her there to himself. He made a mental note to tell her he would pick her up. He didn't want Duke bringing her to his place in the limo and then hanging out until after dinner to take her home. No, Wyatt wanted her all to himself after the family left.

He wondered what she and Ernie were seeing and what Ernie was telling her. He suspected a historic tour of Verity had new sights to see. The tour probably would keep Ernie busy for the next two hours.

His phone rang and caller ID indicated Jake Calhoun.

"So you're back," he said.

"Yes, we are." It was Madison who answered.

"You sound happy."

"I am, Wyatt. Happier than I've ever been." She paused to take a breath. "So I hear you've met Destiny Jones. We weren't here when she came to town, but she said she met you."

"Oh, yes. You've talked to Destiny?"

"Yes. That's why I'm calling. She called me this morning and asked me for an interview this afternoon at two o'clock. She's heard about the Milan-Calhoun feud and she wants to talk about it."

Wyatt shook his head. "Damn. I told her no interview with me. She hasn't said a word to me about any Milan-Calhoun interview with you today and I just saw her. She didn't tell me she would ask other members of my family." His hand tightened on the phone. He had known she would stir up trouble over the feud. He'd been right about that from the start.

"Well, I'm sorry, but evidently, you're not going to get interviewed by Ms. Jones," Madison said and he could hear the laughter in her voice, which added to his annoyance.

"I don't want to be interviewed, dammit. I've turned her down on an interview. I don't want her to stir up that old feud. With your marriage to Jake, things are smoothing over a bit between the families. We don't need a stranger to sail into town and fan the flames of old angers and bad feelings."

"Maybe she'll just talk about how the feud is over and how happy a Milan can be married to a Calhoun." Madison's smile was audible.

"She didn't come to Texas to get background for a show of sweetness and light."

"She'll interview Jake and me, and I think she is calling one of his siblings and maybe another one of mine. Obviously, it's not you. I thought I'd give you a heads-up."

"Thank you for that," Wyatt said. "Any chance of getting you to back out of it?"

"I don't think so. Why should I? It's an old story that everyone around here knows, so what's the harm?"

"I just figure it may stir up hard feelings."

"I won't do that and neither will Jake. Especially since we just got married," she said, the tone of her voice softening. He was happy for her and didn't want to intrude on that happiness or spoil even a fraction of it.

"Sure. When and where is this interview—at Jake's ranch or yours?"

"Neither. I've moved into Jake's home on his ranch, but the interview is in Verity. It's in the Verity Hotel lobby," she replied. "You can come observe if you'd like."

He wanted to groan. "I should have known. Thank you for the heads-up. When she came to town she drew a crowd and had an impromptu press conference that got reporters here from as far away as Dallas. They must have been coming to Verity anyway or got a chopper here. Get ready for a lot of attention. Have you seen her yet?"

"No. She said I can't miss her—she has red curly hair. So do a lot of other people, but I'll find her."

"Madison, you couldn't miss her if you were blind. You'll smell her perfume, hear her jewelry clinking, hear her laughter. No one else in Texas looks like her."

"Am I talking to Wyatt Milan?"

"Very funny."

"Well, now I'm interested in meeting her. Really interested. I've never heard you give that much description of a woman."

"As sheriff I've learned to be more observant," he remarked, knowing his sister was teasing him. "I'll be there with my deputy. Do your best to convey that the feud is over."

"I will. All she has to do is look at me with Jake."

"I'm sure that's the truth. Now, on another subject—how about you and Jake come for dinner Friday night at my place? Nick and Tony want to meet Destiny, although now they'll get to if they come watch this interview, but they want to get to talk to her."

"Friday night is fine with me. I'll check with Jake and let you know."

"Good. See you this afternoon."

He ended the call and swore quietly, getting up and going to the lobby where Dwight was at his desk, typing on his computer.

"If you want to let your wife know, Destiny Jones is going to interview members of my family at the Verity Hotel this afternoon at two o'clock. That will draw another crowd."

"She's a busy woman. She'll put Verity on the map."

"Yeah, well, I'm not sure Verity wants to be on the map." Wyatt rubbed his neck. "She's interviewing my family about the feud."

"Oh, my. Which one? Nick?"

"No, Madison and Jake Calhoun. Who knows who else, but she sure as hell didn't ask me to give her an okay to do this." Wyatt thought his deputy looked as if he tried to hide a laugh.

"I'm sure she didn't. You would have killed the interview."

"Yes, I would have." He left and heard his cell phone ring.

When he answered, it was his brother Tony. "I know you've already talked to Madison. I thought I'd tell you two things. One, thanks for the dinner invitation and I'll be there Friday night."

"Great. You'll have a chance to talk to her at length. Now, what else?"

"She called me and I have an interview with her this afternoon at the Verity Hotel about the feud."

"Would it do me any good to ask you to try to avoid stirring up trouble? That feud is beginning to die a natural death. Don't bring it back to life."

"I'll try not to, Wyatt, but I know she's also interviewing Lindsay Calhoun, so don't expect too much."

"Oh, dammit, Tony. You and Lindsay fight constantly. The two of you will fan the flames of this old feud until it's blazing away again."

"I'll try to soften my answers, but she better lay off antagonizing me."

"If she antagonizes you, try to save up telling her off until you're away from a microphone and far away from Destiny."

"I'll keep that in mind."

"Tony, don't make things worse," Wyatt said.

"Okay, okay. Are you going to be there?"

"Wouldn't miss it for the world."

"See you then," Tony said right before he hung up. Once again Wyatt swore quietly. He walked back to the lobby.

"I called my wife. She's coming for the interview."

"Yeah, and everyone else in town, including all the Milans and the Calhouns. I don't want it to turn into a circus. Destiny doesn't have a calming effect on people. If I can just keep my family calm, hopefully, Jake or one of the Calhouns will keep a cool head. It damn well won't be Lindsay or Tony." Wyatt shook his head and left, walking across the street in long strides as he headed to the Verity Hotel.

Without stopping at the desk, Wyatt went to Destiny's suite and knocked.

In minutes she opened the door and her eyes widened when she faced him. "Come in, I think." She stepped back as he entered.

"I thought it was Amy or Duke or Virginia at the door. I didn't even look out," Destiny said.

"Maybe you should be more careful."

"Come in," she said, leading the way into the living area. His blue eyes were as dark as a stormy sky and she could feel his disapproval when she opened the door. "Have a seat, Wyatt," she said, sitting on a corner of the sofa and folding one leg beneath her. The look of fury had lessened and now he had a faint smile playing at the corners of his mouth. Puzzled at the change in him, she wondered why he was here. He sat near the center of the sofa, not far from her. Her gaze dropped to his mouth while memories of his kisses made her conscious of how close he sat.

"So this is the way you sit around the house when you're just hanging out?" he asked.

She looked down at her designer clothes. She wore lounging slacks and a silk top in bold black-and-white stripes and high-heeled black sandals.

"Sometimes," she said. "When I travel I see others

whom I don't know or don't know well. Sometimes it pays to be dressed decently. Like right now."

"I don't know about 'decently.' What you do for that outfit—I'd describe it in a different way."

"I know you didn't come here to check out what I'm wearing."

"I sure as hell didn't," Wyatt said. "Did you know you're getting ready to do something that will hurt my family and maybe a lot of people?"

"Wyatt, you and I have different views of the world. I'm not trying to hurt your family or anyone else. The feud is interesting and I'm not going to rekindle it with my questions. Your sister married a Calhoun. If anything this should show the town and the state that feuds can be resolved—time passes and they die. Now, what's wrong with that?"

"If you were just interviewing Madison and Jake, I would not be as concerned. You're interviewing Tony and Lindsay who despise each other and fight on a weekly basis in every way they can."

"Is that right? Just because those two can't get along, it isn't going to start the feud up again. Besides, it obviously has never completely died. It's just news and interesting. If I don't write about it, sooner or later someone else will."

"I'd rather take that chance and maybe it would be way later and not even matter so much when there are Milan-Calhoun descendants who have blood from both families."

"You're worrying for nothing. Sheriff Milan, take the afternoon off, go fishing, enjoy life and you won't know the difference tomorrow."

"So you're going ahead with the interview?"

"That's what I came to Verity to do, and you're not giving me a valid reason to cancel it, so yes, I'm going to interview your sister, who is very nice and friendly. She didn't seem worried about having an interview."

"She is just back from her short honeymoon. She isn't going to worry about anything right now. The whole world is a rosy place and she is deliriously happy."

"How nice. Well, that should come across in the interview. Relax, Wyatt. I'm not going to stir up a generations-old feud."

He turned away, not answering her, and she sat in silence studying his profile, wishing he wasn't angry with her. But he was being ridiculous about an ancient family feud. Through the years, it seemed to have turned more into a legend, and while her grandmother didn't have kind words for the Milans, she really hadn't ever been involved with one.

Finally, he stood. "All right, Destiny. I'll be back at two o'clock just to make sure everything stays quiet and peaceful."

As she stood, she faced him. "I really think you'd be happier if you would go fishing, play golf, ride a horse or whatever it is that you enjoy doing."

His expression changed, one corner of his mouth lifting slightly as he stepped closer. "You know what I enjoy doing most?" he asked in a husky voice that warmed her insides and changed their conversation.

"You know what I meant, Wyatt. Something fun you like."

"I'm talking about the most fun possible and what I like most." The deep tone of his voice seemed to caress her as his hands would have. She tingled and lost her train of thought for a moment.

"I'll be happy to have you in the audience," she whispered finally. "As a matter of fact, would you like me to ask you to say a few words from your perspective about the family feud?"

He stepped closer to her, making her heart race. She tried to keep from looking at his mouth and thinking about

YOUR PARTICIPATION IS REQUESTED!

Dear Reader,

Since you are a lover of our books – we would like to get to know you!

Inside you will find a short Reader's Survey. Sharing your answers with us will help our editorial staff understand who you are and what activities you enjoy.

To thank you for your participation, we would like to send you 2 books and 2 gifts – **ABSOLUTELY FREE!**

Enjoy your gifts with our appreciation,

Pam Powers

SEE INSIDE FOR READER'S SURVEY

For Your Reading Pleasure...

We'll send you 2 books and 2 gifts
ABSOLUTELY FREE
just for completing our Reader's Survey!

YOUR READER'S SURVEY
"THANK YOU" FREE GIFTS INCLUDE:
- ▶ 2 FREE books
- ▶ 2 lovely surprise gifts

▶ DETACH AND MAIL CARD TODAY!

PLEASE FILL IN THE CIRCLES COMPLETELY TO RESPOND

1) What type of fiction books do you enjoy reading? (Check all that apply)
- ○ Suspense/Thrillers   ○ Action/Adventure   ○ Modern-day Romances
- ○ Historical Romance   ○ Humour   ○ Paranormal Romance

2) What attracted you most to the last fiction book you purchased on impulse?
- ○ The Title   ○ The Cover   ○ The Author   ○ The Story

3) What is usually the greatest influencer when you <u>plan</u> to buy a book?
- ○ Advertising   ○ Referral   ○ Book Review

4) How often do you access the internet?
- ○ Daily   ○ Weekly   ○ Monthly   ○ Rarely or never

5) How many NEW paperback fiction novels have you purchased in the past 3 months?
- ○ 0 - 2   ○ 3 - 6   ○ 7 or more

YES! I have completed the Reader's Survey. Please send me the 2 FREE books and 2 FREE gifts (gifts are worth about $10) for which I qualify. I understand that I am under no obligation to purchase any books, as explained on the back of this card.

225/326 HDL GGCS

FIRST NAME	LAST NAME

ADDRESS

| APT.# | CITY |

| STATE/PROV. | ZIP/POSTAL CODE |

EMAIL

Offer limited to one per household and not applicable to series that subscriber is currently receiving.
Your Privacy—The Harlequin Reader Service is committed to protecting your privacy. Our Privacy Policy is available online at www.ReaderService.com or upon request from the Harlequin Reader Service. We make a portion of our mailing list available to reputable third parties that offer products we believe may interest you. If you prefer that we not exchange your name with third parties, or if you wish to clarify or modify your communication preferences, please visit us at www.ReaderService.com/consumerschoice or write to us at Harlequin Reader Service Preference Service, P.O. Box 9062, Buffalo, NY 14240-9062. Include your complete name and address.

© 2014 HARLEQUIN ENTERPRISES LIMITED
® and ™ are trademarks owned and used by the trademark owner and/or its licensee. Printed in the U.S.A.

HD-914-SUR-13

HARLEQUIN READER SERVICE — Here's How It Works:

kisses. "You ask me anything about the family feud and you'll regret bringing it up. I'll be so damn dull, I'll kill your interview."

Her smile broadened. "I do believe I've pierced our sheriff's laid-back armor, that 'nothing ever really disturbs me' attitude."

"Watch out, Destiny," he said in a low voice.

"Now you're giving me a challenge. You think you can dull my interview? It might be worth it just to try to break through that impenetrable cool attitude you carry off in the face of all kinds of turmoil."

"If you want to break through my laid-back attitude, there's a far easier way to do so," he said.

Her smile faded. He stood as close as he could without touching her. His eyes were no longer dark blue with anger, but had transformed to crystal blue with a heavy-lidded gaze that held blatant desire. His attention shifted lower to her mouth and her lips parted. Without thought, she leaned toward him a fraction, pressing against him, and his arm circled her waist. He pulled her up against him and leaned down to kiss her, his mouth hard and demanding, his kiss passionate. His other hand tangled in her hair, sending pins and the ribbon flying, causing locks to fall over her shoulders.

He leaned over her and she held him tightly, clinging to him while she moaned, wanting him desperately. His hand slid over her, caressing her, freeing buttons, and he shoved the top open to cup her breast in his hand. Her small cry of pleasure seemed to come from far away. She held Wyatt, sliding one hand over his muscled shoulders and chest, kissing him wantonly, desiring him with all her being. How could he do this to her so effortlessly?

"Wyatt, the bedroom," she whispered.

Never breaking contact with her lips, he picked her up. She didn't open her eyes, but was lost in his kisses. She felt him carrying her, not caring what was happening as long as she was in his arms and he was kissing her.

As he stood her on her feet, his hands caressed her breasts. "You're so beautiful. All I can think about is you," he whispered and leaned down to kiss her breast while his hand slipped beneath the silk pants and he stroked her between her thighs.

She gasped and held his shoulders while writhing with need. With an urgency that made her hands tremble she peeled away his brown shirt and trailed kisses over his chest as she undid his belt and then his uniform slacks, pushing them off his narrow hips.

After he picked her up to place her on the bed, he turned away to get protection.

"Wyatt, come to me," she whispered, running her hands over his muscled thighs.

"I wanted you, Destiny." He lowered himself between her legs and entered her, filling her in one smooth motion, moving slowly while she thrashed beneath him.

Wanting him with her whole being, she scaled the peak quickly, bursting with release, enveloped in ecstasy. He pumped faster, until seconds later she felt him shudder. His arms wrapped around her, pressing her close while they still moved together, even after they were sated.

"Wyatt, if only I could just hold this moment forever," she whispered more to herself than to him. He showered light kisses on her cheek and temple and rolled on his side, keeping her close so they faced each other.

"Ah, Destiny. You're fantastic," he whispered, combing curly strands of red hair away from her face. "Beautiful."

"You did this, Wyatt, to make me late for my interview," she said lightly.

His hand stilled and for an instant she wondered if that was exactly what he had done.

"I made love to you because you came to the door in

clothes that clung to you like a second skin and your big, green eyes held desire while your kisses were an invitation. Tell me you didn't want to make love."

She looked into the bluest eyes she had ever seen. "You know I wanted to," she whispered. "So did you." Like an intruder, reality broke through her thoughts. "Wyatt, I can't stay here in bed. A crew will be arriving shortly to set up so I can record the interview."

"This interview will be televised, won't it?"

"Not today. Not live. It will be taped and whether it's aired will depend on other things, my stay in Verity, my story about Verity. The interview may go into archives and never be heard of again, so cheer up. Few may ever even know about it, but I have to get ready and get downstairs, so you, Sheriff Milan, are going to have to dress and go."

He kissed her long and passionately and then released her. "I'll go, but you won't forget our time together, our making love." He stepped out of bed. "I'll get dressed in your guest bathroom." He picked up his things as she gathered hers and headed for her shower.

When she came out, Wyatt had gone.

At ten minutes before two o'clock, Wyatt entered the hotel lobby. Destiny was nowhere in sight, nor was there anyone else present who would be involved in the interview, which made him wonder if she had followed his urging and canceled it.

He was beginning to feel better and pleased with her when he spotted a sign on a pedestal as he approached the elevators. The sign directed anyone interested in the Milan-Calhoun interview to go to the second-floor central ballroom.

He headed for the stairs and on the second floor when he passed through open double doors into the large ball-

room, Wyatt spotted Destiny instantly as she stood looking at a sheaf of papers in her hands.

Potted plants had been moved to a corner, five chairs
were set up in the front of the room, lit by TV lights and
framed by cameras whose wires snaked across the polished
hotel floor. Briefly he wondered where she got the camera crew, when all she'd brought to Verity was Virginia
Boyden. His pulse quickened and he wanted to go talk to
her, but he knew she was working now and her thoughts
would be on the interview.

Looking sophisticated, Destiny had her hair looped and
pinned on the top and back of her head, yet he couldn't
keep from remembering all that red hair spilled over her
bare shoulders and breasts less than a couple of hours earlier. She was in a blue dress that clung to her figure and
had a V neckline—another dress that would turn heads.
Watching her, he felt a mixture of emotions—annoyance
that she would do the interview and desire to be with her
the rest of the day and night, which he knew was impos-
sible. He had wanted peace and quiet—something that
had settled over Verity since he took office and he trea-
sured it in the town and in his own life. Now his world
was churning and he could feel trouble boiling beneath
the surface, ready to bubble up at any time with Destiny's
troublemaking.

People were beginning to gather and some had even
brought their own chairs. There was a buzz of conversation among the people, who looked as if they were at a
party with eagerness and expectation in their expressions.
When Wyatt spotted his sister and new brother-in-law, he
went over to greet them.

He walked up to Madison, giving her a hug. "Welcome
home, Mrs. Calhoun."

Hugging him in return, Madison laughed. "That makes
me feel as if I should look around for Jake's mother."

"Hi, Jake. You've been able to put up with her for a while now," Wyatt said, shaking hands with his new brother-in-law.

"I don't view her quite the same way as her brothers do," he remarked, hugging her against him and keeping his arm around her. Madison smiled and stuck her tongue out at Wyatt.

"So there, brother, dear," she said sweetly. "We go on first and I will tell about the legend and how it's faded to almost nothing."

"Definitely nothing," Jake said. "I'm friends with all of you and in love with one of the Milans. No feud there." Jake smiled at Madison who smiled up at him. In that instance they were wrapped in their own world, their happiness obvious. Looking at them, Wyatt thought of Katherine and the marriage he had hoped and expected to have, and probably the children they would have had by now. He closed his mind on those memories. His eyes lit on Destiny and his ache vanished, replaced by memories of their lovemaking a couple of hours earlier, holding Destiny in his arms as he kissed her, her softness and warmth.

Sometime later he realized Madison was talking. "...then at some point, she will interview Lindsay and Tony. That's what you should worry about, not when I talk about marrying Jake," she said, smiling at her new husband, who brushed a light kiss on her cheek. "See— no feud between us. It's dead forever. I love the Calhouns, particularly one of them."

Wyatt had to laugh. "I think I'll go say hi to Tony. You two need your own island. Don't start smooching on television."

"I'll try to remember," she said, without taking her gaze from Jake.

Wyatt smiled and walked away, strolling up to Tony, who looked just what he was—a Texas rancher. He wore a blue Western shirt, his wide-brimmed black hat, jeans and boots. His belt was wider than Wyatt's and the silver belt buckle larger. Wyatt shook hands with his brother.

"Please don't get people really stirred up," he told Tony. "There are a lot of people around with Calhoun blood even if their name isn't Calhoun."

"I know. I won't. I'll be civil if the little witch will button her lips."

"Please don't call her 'the little witch.' I want to avoid stirring up old feelings or making this feud any worse than it currently is. You and Lindsay Calhoun fan the flames constantly and keep this feud alive more than any other Milans or Calhouns."

"Maybe so, but there's damn good reason. She is a pestiferous— There isn't a word to describe her except *witch*."

Wyatt groaned. "Try to avoid it for the next three hours. I want peace and quiet in here and no fistfights."

"Okay, for you, I will. And because I have a dinner invitation to your house this week to meet Destiny Jones. She is one good-looking woman," Tony said, his face taking on a dazed expression as he sought out the lady in question. Wyatt, too, turned to look at her again.

"That is as true as Texas," Wyatt said, forgetting his brother and thinking about Destiny. He had plans for Friday night that went beyond the dinner he was hosting for his brothers. For him, it was a means to an end. He couldn't wait to be alone with her again.

"Here comes Nick," Tony said. He greeted his brother when Nick joined him and shook hands with Wyatt.

"I have to go," Tony said. "Destiny is motioning me over. I'm most happy to do whatever she wants. See you guys."

Wyatt turned to Nick. "Well, you and I are just spectators to this unless something's changed during the past hour," he said.

"That suits me fine. I'm impressed with her ability to deal with a crowd and her ability to draw a crowd. I can't tell you how much I'd like to hire her for my PR person. She would be fantastic in that position."

She's fantastic in all sorts of positions, Wyatt thought. He sighed, wishing this would be over quickly and he could have some time alone with her again.

He scanned the room, noticing that the number of people had risen considerably since his arrival.

Nick slapped him on the back. "Relax, Sheriff. There hasn't been an actual fight between a Milan and a Calhoun since—"

"Not since a month ago when Lindsay dumped a truckload of manure on one of Tony's ranch roads."

Nick grinned. "Those two are your troublemakers. He did something to provoke her, you can bet on that."

Knowing Nick was right, Wyatt strolled away, greeting the new arrivals and making his presence known. He was certain Nick was right—fights would not break out—but it was a crowd and there were a few strong feelings, although he suspected Destiny could keep a crowd under control with the greatest of ease.

One half of the ballroom was already filled and Wyatt kept moving. He knew it would be like this. The audience had grown steadily and now that it was nearing time to start, more and more people had come. He saw people who worked for Lindsay and some who worked for Tony.

Finally, Destiny took her seat in a chair facing the audience. A small table was beside her and it held some papers, a pitcher of ice water and paper cups. Madison and Jake sat nearby, angled to one side, yet where they could see both the audience and Destiny.

Wyatt looked at his sister, who was wearing a navy suit and matching blouse and heels, a far more tailored look than she usually had. He swore she almost had a glow

about her; the faint smile and starry-eyed look she gave
Jake as he sat close beside her conveyed her bliss, which
made Wyatt happy for her. Jake was a good guy and Wyatt
was glad they were finally married. He hoped the past was
really behind them.

Rising, Destiny opened the program. "Folks, thanks for
your interest today. I'm Destiny Jones. I have a show orig-
inating in Chicago, which I hope all of you watch, called
Unsolved Mysteries." She smiled while the onlookers applauded, led by Jake, who was facing everyone. "Thank
you to all who enjoy the show. Some of the mysteries we
attempt to solve on the show date back to another century and that's what has brought me to the unique town
of Verity, Texas."

She waited for more applause from the crowd.

"I'm interested in three unsolved murders from years
ago. Two of the men killed one spring night several generations ago were Mortimer Milan and Reuben Calhoun.

"As I understand the history here, almost since the first
few days they settled in this area, the Milans and the Calhouns have been feuding, blaming each other for all sorts
of trouble. For a lot of years, members of each family
would not speak to members of the other family.

"Today, that feud may be dying out because now we
have a Milan and a Calhoun who have married and so the
families are brought together and hereafter will be related."

As the audience applauded, Jake took Madison's hand
and smiled at her.

When they quieted, Destiny continued, "Folks, I'm
guessing everyone in the room knows both of these people—Mr. and Mrs. Jake Calhoun." There was more enthusiastic applause.

"I'm sure all of you from Verity already know Mrs.
Jake Calhoun is Madison Milan, so now these two famous
families are joined."

Destiny took her seat and as she continued talking about Verity and Texas legends, Wyatt stepped back and watched the crowd. Everyone seemed interested, sat quietly and attentively and he relaxed a bit. To his relief, he knew the majority of the people who were present.

Destiny gave a lively talk and then asked Jake to tell about the feud as he knew it from the Calhoun point of view.

Looking relaxed, dressed in a navy shirt, jeans and boots, Jake took Madison's hand again, smiling at her, and Wyatt had another surge of relief that Jake was on camera because he was levelheaded and obviously in love with a Milan.

"I've heard the legend as far back as my memory goes. It's two early-day families—both with big families that included aunts, uncles, grandparents, mothers, fathers and brothers who settled here. According to all the stories, there were several things that contributed to trouble between the Calhouns and the Milans. The land they staked out and claimed for each ranch shared the same border. Calhouns and Milans were neighbors with the same creeks running across both ranches so water became an issue between them. They didn't have fences at first, so they fought over cattle. There weren't as many women out on the frontier, so the men fought over their women. There were other problems, too—Milans claimed that a Calhoun bet and lost part of the Calhoun land to the Milans in a card game. The battle continued through the years as this area settled and became more civilized. Gradually, some Milans began to speak to some Calhouns and some Calhouns began to speak to some Milans. And now," he said, pausing to smile at Madison, "one Calhoun has married a Milan and there is no feud as far as the two of us are concerned. I hope the old feud is over forever."

The audience clapped, but Jake noticed neither Tony nor Lindsay clapped.

Destiny quieted the crowd. "Madison, we haven't heard from you. Is that about the way you've always been told about the legend?"

"Yes, it is," she said, smiling at Jake. "Just about the same. Both families did things to the other one and from what I've always been told, the biggest fights have involved water and, I have to admit, women. The Milan-Calhoun feud is definitely over as far as we're concerned. I hope both our families are at peace with each other from now on."

Destiny smiled at the audience as they applauded Madison's statement.

"So maybe the end of the feud has come," Destiny said, smiling at the audience. She stood, moving freely with a lapel mike. "As all of you can see there are Milans and Calhouns in the audience this afternoon and everyone is peaceful, so it looks as if Jake and Madison are right and the feud is over and another Texas legend goes into the local history books."

The audience again applauded.

"Do any of the Milans or Calhouns want to come forward and add anything?"

Wyatt held his breath and glanced at Tony to see him standing at the edge of the crowd, his arms folded. He looked relaxed, mildly interested and not on the verge of moving. Wyatt was about to let out his breath when a hand went up and he wanted to groan out loud.

"Ah, someone has her hand in the air and we met right before I started taping," Destiny said. "It's Lindsay Calhoun, right?"

"That's right," Lindsay said. Wyatt had moments when he had to admire Lindsay because she was a competent rancher and had the respect of most all the ranchers in the area. She was another woman who didn't scare easily. He just wished both Lindsay and Tony would be more tolerant and cooperative and try to work out their disputes.

At the moment he wanted to grit his teeth and he braced for what was coming next.

"Come up here, Lindsay, and join your brother if you have something to add."

Jake stood, but he didn't applaud when the audience did. Even though he had a faint smile, he looked about as solemn as Wyatt felt.

Wyatt noticed that Madison made no attempt to hug her new sister-in-law or greet her in any way except with a smile.

With her blond hair in a long braid, and dressed in a long-sleeve green Western shirt and jeans, Lindsay took the empty chair Destiny motioned her to, as well as the handheld mike she offered.

"So, Lindsay, do you agree with your brother that the feud is over?" Destiny asked, once she was again seated.

"It definitely is for Jake and Madison, which is nice," she said, smiling at Jake and then turning to face the crowd. "I'm not so sure it is for all Calhouns and Milans," she stated. Someone in the audience whistled, while another man said, "Tell 'em, Lindsay."

Lindsay laughed. "Not all Calhouns and Milans get along like my brother and his new wife, so I don't think anyone can say the feud is over."

"Can you give me a modern-day example?" Destiny asked. "Why would any Calhoun be annoyed with any Milan, or vice versa?"

"Well, some of us are still ranchers and some of us still have neighboring ranches and that can set up a situation to be as volatile as it was a century ago. If someone lets their cattle overgraze a field, or diverts a creek, or dumps manure over a fence," she added, her voice getting a harsher tone, "then tempers flare." There was a smattering of applause and Lindsay smiled at the audience. "See, my feelings are shared."

"From my perspective," Jake said, "some Calhouns and some Milans are a little touchier than others. Time is against this feud and it's fading. I think Lindsay will have to agree that in our lifetime it's changed and not taken as seriously by as many family members as it used to be."

There was more applause for Jake, who smiled at the audience and then at his sister.

"I agree," Lindsay offered. "I'm just saying it isn't over as long as one family does something to someone from the other family. And that continues to happen. The day that stops between all Calhouns and Milans, then I'll agree the feud is over."

"There are cousins, aunts, uncles, members of both families, the Milans and the Calhouns, who have moved away from Verity," Destiny said. "For them this feud no longer exists, so would all of you agree that it's limited to Verity and family members who have ranches in this vicinity?"

Jake and Madison replied yes, but Lindsay shook her head. "No, I can't agree," she said. "There are Milans and Calhouns who live in Dallas and other Texas cities and I know they don't speak if they meet members of the other family."

"Are you and your neighbor on speaking terms?" Destiny asked.

"Only when we have to be or when either of us can't resist sounding off. Otherwise, we don't speak."

"So the feud is still alive. Do you think the feud goes beyond just local Milans and Calhouns?"

"I think it does," Lindsay replied.

"I guess I'll test out your theory, Lindsay," Destiny said. "I haven't been in Verity long, but I've been welcomed by all I've met, Milans and Calhouns, and I hope that doesn't change, but I can add my own background to this discussion."

Suddenly Wyatt's attention focused on Destiny and he forgot the crowd. Her gaze met his, but with the bright lights, he doubted whether she could really see him.

"I was born in Houston, Texas," she said and paused while there was applause from some of the onlookers. "My family on my mother's side was Calhouns."

Six

Shocked again by Destiny, Wyatt frowned. Why hadn't she told him? Stunned, annoyed. One after the other, the emotions battered Wyatt as he watched her. There was applause and Destiny walked closer to the crowd gathered to watch her while she still gazed at Wyatt.

She had rocked his world from the first moment he had spotted the red limo. So far, this was the biggest jolt of all and his annoyance transformed to a simmering anger. She was a paradox to him—physically intimate with him, yet holding back this vital information about herself until she decided to tell the whole town. Why hadn't she told him that she was a Calhoun, especially since she knew he'd been upset about her interviews because of the feud?

Instantly, he guessed she had waited for the biggest impact by announcing it during this interview. From the first second he should have realized she waited for the biggest public relations impact.

His anger eased only slightly because she still could

have told him and let him know that she would announce it this afternoon.

He folded his arms and stared at her while he absorbed the news that he had been in bed with a Calhoun. Again, he recalled the first moment he had seen the red limo in his parking spot and her in his office. He had known she would cause trouble in his peaceful town and his quiet life. She had proven him right over and over and this was a crowning touch—except he suspected the worst was still to come.

He watched Destiny in the front of the ballroom, calm and professional as she continued. "I was never caught up in the feud because my mother wasn't. I knew nothing about it until we moved to California when I was a teen and I was told by my grandmother, who has strong feelings about being a Calhoun," she said. "My heritage gives me a personal interest in the feud now."

She smiled at Lindsay. "I'm looking forward to meeting more of my Calhoun relatives."

"Jake and I'll be happy to introduce you," Lindsay said, smiling in return.

Destiny stepped forward, closer to her audience. "Since we've heard from Lindsay Calhoun, I think in all fairness, we should give her neighbor a chance to speak because he's in our audience—if he's willing to come forward. Tony Milan?" She looked at the audience.

Wyatt groaned. For a moment he hoped Tony had left, but then he saw his brother walking up to the front of the room, turning to the audience and saying, "I'll guarantee you, I'm speaking to this Calhoun. I have no quarrel with her," he said as he took Destiny's hand. "Welcome to Verity."

Wyatt noticed that everyone applauded except Lindsay. Jake said something to his sister and she shook her head.

"Thank you," Destiny said. "Sit and join us. Do you have anything to add to what Lindsay has told us?"

"She's covered it all," he said, still smiling as he pulled his chair a few inches away from Lindsay and sat.

Wyatt felt it was too soon to yield to the relief he was beginning to feel. He was proud of Tony for keeping the situation light and upbeat and placing Destiny in a position that might make her want to cooperate. Tony and Lindsay had not looked at each other. If he just kept his cool, the interview would move on.

"As big as these ranches are, I wouldn't think you would ever get in each other's way," Destiny said and Tony simply shrugged and smiled while Lindsay gazed solemnly at Destiny.

"Texas isn't big enough to avoid this clash," Lindsay said quietly, but some in the audience heard and laughed.

"You don't have anything to add to this?" Destiny asked Tony.

"I'm sitting between my new Calhoun brother-in-law and the beautiful Calhoun star and host of the television show, *Unsolved Mysteries,* so no, I'm not causing a ripple with Calhouns today," Tony said with a big grin and got a round of applause that Wyatt joined.

Destiny laughed. "I might move back to Texas," she said to the audience and smiled at Tony. The audience responded with hearty cheers.

"Move to Verity," someone yelled and she waved. Destiny smiled, looking at the audience. Wyatt had drifted slowly until he was standing near a cameraman. As she talked, Destiny looked directly into Wyatt's eyes.

"Since I've been here, I've met Milans and Calhouns and I like them all, so I see no reason for a feud to continue. I wish you happiness and an end to the feud," she said to Jake and Madison.

She turned to the audience. "So that's the history and

the story of a Texas feud from generations ago until the present day. Thank you, Lindsay, Madison, Jake and Tony. Thank all of you for stopping to join us and your gracious hospitality to me and my staff."

While the lights dimmed and the taping broke up. Destiny turned to talk to her guests while people from the audience began to line up to talk to her.

Wyatt let out his breath and moved to the edge of the crowd, stepping back, waiting to make sure everyone left without a problem. He walked to Tony. "Thank you and I'm proud you could resist coming back at her."

"I wanted to, but I figured the entire family would be relieved if I didn't and Madison is so happy right now—I don't want to do one thing to toss a damper on her joy."

"So maybe my little brother is growing up. That's good, Tony, because I know Lindsay is no saint."

"Don't get me started, Wyatt."

"I wouldn't think of it. I'm glad you can come to dinner Friday night."

"I'd like that." He glanced around the room. "Lindsay's talking to Destiny. I'll get out while everything is smooth. I don't care to join in any conversation that Lindsay is part of. If I do, Destiny might see the bad side of the feud come to life."

"See you Friday night and thanks again for averting more trouble." He watched his younger brother turn and leave the ballroom and he was proud of Tony. The room was emptying fast. Wyatt started to join Destiny, but Nick stepped in front of him.

"It went better than I expected," Nick said. "Still wish I could hire her."

Wyatt smiled. "Won't happen. Even for money, I don't think she would give up the limelight. She's a natural for the work she does."

"Yes, she is. I have to run now or I'm going to be late for an appointment, but I'll see you Friday night."

"Great."

"I was proud of Tony."

"He is growing up, Nick. He held it in and I know it took an effort."

"Amen. He surprised me because those two have strong feelings between them. See you," Nick said over his shoulder as he headed toward the door and was gone.

Wyatt moved on, hanging back until Lindsay turned to leave. He looked into her blue eyes. A Calhoun without brown eyes, he thought.

"Hi, Lindsay," he said.

"Wyatt," she answered coolly and he was surprised she even bothered to acknowledge him because most of the time she didn't. She hurried past him and out of sight.

He waited while Destiny finished talking to the camera crew and to Amy. She strolled over to Wyatt.

"Destiny Calhoun, that was a surprise," he said. "I suppose you waited for the most dramatic moment to break that news around here. Why didn't you tell me earlier?"

"It surely wouldn't have made a difference, would it?"

"Not at all," he answered. "It would have been nicer not to get it cold like I did. Maybe this way I felt shut out of your life even more than I am."

Something flickered in the depths of her eyes. "That does surprise me. What we have is a lusty, physical attraction with no future to it. I never thought about either of us getting closer otherwise. You keep part of yourself locked away all the time."

"I suppose I do," he said quietly. "Maybe today for a brief time I got closer and in the euphoria from that feeling, your announcement emphasized that I had made a mistake."

"Other than physically, I don't think we were one degree closer today," she said solemnly. "You just didn't like being surprised. You haven't shared your past with me or lost one bit of that wall you keep around yourself. I didn't think you'd care when I let you know my heritage, and I got a little drama out of announcing it when I did."

"You got your interview and it went better than I expected," he said, wanting to drop the discussion of deepening their relationship. That wasn't going to happen.

"Your brother is a charmer and it's a stretch to imagine him fighting with anyone, much less someone as pretty as Lindsay Calhoun," Destiny said.

"Tony has his moments. So where did you get all the camera crew?"

"An affiliate in Dallas." She checked her watch. "Shortly, I have an appointment to talk to one of your local historians—Gilda who works in the Verity Historical Museum."

"Gilda can tell you the history of this place. She'll be more informative than the little museum. She knows more about Verity and the people here than anyone else in town." He shifted his weight while he gazed into Destiny's expressive green eyes that relayed desire.

"Well, I was hoping we could go back to your room and finish what we started," he said, wanting to touch her, but resisting because of the people moving around them.

"I thought we did finish what we started."

"Hardly. I'll show you next time I get the opportunity." He resisted the urge to do so now, though he did lean a little closer to her. "I'm glad you did the interview because that's what caused me to go to the hotel to talk to you."

"I don't see any chance to really be with you until Friday night."

"I'll pick you up Friday night. That way I'll get to talk to you because once we get to my house, my brothers are going to take all your time."

She smiled at him. "Fine. I see Amy headed my way. I'd better get back to work."

"Okay, see you Friday," he said, leaving the ballroom and feeling Destiny watching him walk out.

Wyatt left for the office, but he didn't feel like dealing with business. He was thinking about his reactions to Destiny. Besides the fantastic sex, he enjoyed being with her and the more he got to know her, the more he wanted to have her with him. She was lively, bringing an enthusiasm for life into any situation she was in. Charm came naturally to her and she charmed everyone around her. She was usually positive, upbeat, filled with life, an extrovert who loved the people she met, interacted easily with them. Destiny was so many things he wasn't, but he liked that about her.

She would only be here a short time and then gone out of his life. He wanted Destiny here longer. The time would come when he'd be ready to tell her goodbye because since his breakup he never got deeply involved, but not this soon. It startled him to realize that he had stronger feelings for Destiny than for anyone since Katherine.

It surprised him even more to realize that he hadn't even thought about Katherine very much in the past two days. After all these years since law school, he usually couldn't get Katherine out of his thoughts—until now. The constant excitement with Destiny would drive everything else out of any man's thoughts. The pain of his breakup was fading more than ever. He was still certain he would never love again the way he had loved Katherine—consequently, he hoped he was never hurt again the way he had been with her—but Destiny was making a difference in his life and he enjoyed her flamboyant style and bubbling enthusiasm, which continually amazed him.

At the door, he glanced over his shoulder and met Destiny's gaze. He left, wondering what her next surprise would be.

* * *

After her last meeting of the day Destiny returned to her suite, tired but pleased with the information she got from the local historian. Changing out of her business clothes, she looked around her bedroom and her thoughts continually drifted to Wyatt and what they had done there earlier that afternoon. She thought about their lovemaking, being in his arms. In his quiet, determined way, he was the most exciting man she had ever known—something she had never expected to feel about him.

Would he ever come to Chicago to see her once she left Verity?

She felt a wishful stab of longing because she knew he wouldn't. Once she left Verity, they would be out of each other's lives forever—if they were ever in each other's lives at all except for the wild, lusty moments of hot sex. That was not enough substance to build a relationship on, she knew, so they would fade into oblivion. She had no illusions about their relationship. It was purely physical, nothing more. At least that had been the way she had viewed it until the past hour when Wyatt had told her he had felt shut out when she didn't tell him she was a Calhoun before the public announcement.

Wyatt's confession had shocked her. It was an indication that he felt something beyond a physical relationship. She knew that his heart was locked away, but maybe there was a crack in that rock wall around his heart. Maybe Wyatt was more vulnerable to deep feelings than he wanted to admit.

There had been a few moments when she had caught a shuttered look in Wyatt's eyes after making love. She felt he had shut his mind to even thinking about their relationship, but his remarks this afternoon indicated otherwise—and made her stop and question how deep her feelings ran for Wyatt.

Destiny shook her head. Wyatt was far more than she

had expected and she responded to him beyond her wildest imaginings. She liked being with him and had to admit he was a calming influence in her life. No matter how much they liked being together, she didn't expect to see him again when she left Verity—unless she returned for the show. She had never been in love in her life and Wyatt wasn't the man to give her heart to because it would be a hopeless love. He may have relented slightly, but he still guarded his heart.

Was she warning herself about him...or was she worrying after the fact? Was she already falling in love?

Was she going home in love with him?

But how could that be? He was not her style at all. She had dated famous men, movie actors, newsmen, dynamic people who moved on the national scene. Wyatt's world was one little town and one sparsely populated county in West Texas, and a ranch filled with cattle. True, he had flown her to Dallas for dinner in a private room, but overall he still led a quiet life. He was controlled, and low-key. He did have a streak of arrogance, expecting to get his way and what he wanted out of life. She had to laugh, though, because she might have a streak of that also. But still, Wyatt Calhoun was the most exciting man she had ever known.

"Sheesh," she said aloud, wondering how he had captured her interest. She couldn't really be in love. When she got back to Chicago, she expected to forget Wyatt fairly fast. At the same time, she liked the way he listened to her, giving her his full attention. She felt he liked her for who she truly was, not a television personality. She felt she could trust him and she understood why the townspeople wanted him for sheriff, because he was honest and trustworthy.

For now, though, she wanted to be in his arms and she wanted his kisses.

The interviews today had been interesting and she had eased off asking Lindsay Calhoun questions that she would have asked if she hadn't known how unhappy Wyatt was with the interview. Lindsay was a spitfire and Destiny knew she could have gotten some good quotes and sound bites out of her. Her nemesis, Tony, on the other hand, was a charmer. So different from his laid-back, laconic older brother.

In some ways, being in Verity County was like stepping back in time. The people here had old-fashioned habits and values, and they'd been incredibly friendly and courteous to her. Just like Wyatt, there was nothing in Verity that she thought would have been her taste but, to her surprise, the quiet little town held an appeal for her. She liked everyone she met and they had welcomed her, again in a sincere way that she felt had nothing to do with her show or her book. The town was refreshing with a relaxed atmosphere and, each day, she could see more of why Wyatt wanted to keep the peace and quiet. In hectic lives, the serenity was a welcome relief. No wonder he liked calling it home.

Shortly, she'd return to her home, Chicago. She'd leave Verity, and Wyatt, behind and return to her life. For some reason, that didn't seem to have the same appeal anymore.

Friday night Wyatt called her from the lobby promptly at seven.

"I'll be up to get you unless you want another grand entrance," he told her. "There is a Verity reporter and one from Lubbock and one from Fort Worth hanging out in the lobby. Word has gotten around that you're a Calhoun, so now they all have a new slant to a story about you. I think I know the answer, but I'll ask, do I come up to get you and we take the private exit?" he asked, sounding amused.

"Of course not. I'll make the grand entrance in the lobby and talk to the reporters. The publicity will be good. I'll get rid of them quickly because I've done this before, although it is easier to escape in the limo, I think. Are you parked at the front?"

"Yes, I am," he said. "Don't worry. When you want to escape, I'll see to it that we escape."

"I have no doubts. I'll bet you think I crave attention as much as Desirée."

"I think you thrive on it," he said and she laughed.

"I like reporters, politicians, even lawyers," she answered.

"Well, now, that's a good thing because you'll be knee-deep in lawyers tonight. And you'll get all their attention, I promise you, especially since you've announced your Calhoun blood."

Her nerves jangled. "Is that going to be a problem for your family?"

"They've already accepted Jake and they can't wait to get to know you, including Tony. I'll guarantee you that being a Calhoun doesn't deter Tony. Your looks overcome your heritage."

She laughed. "I can't wait. I'm coming now. I don't think you'll have any trouble spotting me."

"Oh, I don't think so either. I know I'm going to be dazzled. See you, hon," he said and was gone.

"Hon." She suspected he had thrown that in casually without thought, but it had sent a tingle through her. If only he had meant the emotion it implied, but she knew better.

She picked up her purse, locked up and left, excitement mounting over another evening with Wyatt.

Once again she took the elevator to the second level, stepped off and walked around a corner toward the stairs. The moment the lobby came into view, she saw Wyatt. Tall, dressed in a charcoal suit with a charcoal-and-black tie, a broad-brimmed hat on his head, he stood near the foot of the stairs. His gaze caught hers and she was barely aware in her peripheral vision of reporters and others converging awaiting her.

She couldn't tear her gaze from Wyatt. Tonight she was going to his house to meet part of his family. Tonight the ties between them would grow stronger. She would be in his arms later, sharing kisses, making—

Stop! She practically screamed the command at herself. She had to tear her thoughts from contemplation of what was to come and concentrate on now.

As she started down the steps, photographers and amateurs took her picture. She had long ago learned to descend a staircase while smiling at her audience waiting below.

"Have you talked to your Calhoun relatives who live here, Destiny?" one man called out.

A barrage of questions followed, and she couldn't understand any of them. She paused about five steps from the floor and held up her hand. Instantly, the crowd became silent. She glanced quickly around the lobby once again and saw a few women waiting to see her, holding copies of her book, which gave her a thrill.

Wyatt waited patiently while she answered questions, signed books and finally told the small crowd farewell.

He took her arm and in seconds they were in his car and driving away from the hotel.

"No one follows you," she said with amusement, looking over her shoulder.

"I'm the sheriff. They know me and they have sense enough to know I don't want to be followed. They want my cooperation when something happens, so they cooperate with me. You gave them your time and I waited. Now they're showing some manners and good sense and leaving us alone. This is a town filled with intelligent, kind people."

"You like Verity."

"Of course I do. This is home and these are my friends and relatives."

"They're nice. And Verity has the sexiest sheriff this side of the Atlantic Ocean."

One corner of his mouth curled in a faint smile. "Just wait until tonight and maybe you'll think the whole U.S.A.," he said.

Laughing, she ran her hand over his knee. "When I planned to come to Verity, I never, ever expected to see more of you than just a few moments when I arrived."

"You knew your sister and I saw each other."

"Desirée and I do not attract the same men. Or rather, go out with the same men."

"I can imagine in a way, but most any man would want to go out with either one of you. Looks run in the family."

"Thank you. My mother was the real beauty until her health failed. When I was little, I thought she was the most gorgeous woman in the world."

"That's nice for a little girl to think about her mother."

"She was beautiful. Desirée is, too. Since the day she was born people would stop to look at her. She's the one who looks like our mother. I resemble our grandmother on Mom's side."

"Desirée is one of the most beautiful women I've ever known."

"That's what most men say."

"You're not jealous either," he said, and she shook her head.

"Never. That would be like being jealous of my child. I practically raised her. Besides, I don't have any difficulty attracting men—at least since I reached sixteen. I was the awkward kid until then, too plump, too tall, a mess of unruly curly red hair that I didn't know how to deal with. Desirée was the pretty one."

She turned slightly in the bucket seat to face Wyatt,

comfortable with him, comfortable with talking about her past. "Like I said, our mother was beautiful—at least she was in pictures when she was in her twenties. She never was well after Desirée was born, so I had to help and my grandmother was around a lot. Also, my aunt. She had a son who was my age and like a brother to me." She shrugged. "We fought so much and maybe that's where I lost some of my fear of things, but I also learned a bit about dealing with boys."

"Do you still have your grandmother with you?"

"She's in L.A. and her health is failing. I try to talk to her daily. I love her deeply and we've always been close. She's the one who told me about my Calhoun heritage."

"Do you still see your cousin or your aunt?"

"Sure. They're in L.A., so I don't see them as much as I did when I lived there. He's a director and he's part of the reason Desirée is in the movies."

"You have an interesting family."

"I think you should tell me about your family since we're about to spend the evening with them," she said, studying Wyatt and thinking about later tonight when they would be alone. The thought of making love again started a fizzy current of excitement and anticipation bubbling in her. She wanted to be alone with him again. At the same time, it was one more tie that bound her heart. Wyatt had gotten to her in a way few men had, though she suspected he would forget her within a month after her leaving and he would never feel a pang when she went.

She didn't like to think about telling him goodbye. How could she get even this deeply involved with him in such a short time? She didn't believe in love at first sight—something her sister firmly believed and said had happened with almost every new eligible male she met.

Destiny's gaze roamed over Wyatt's profile and she

wondered what he thought and felt. All she knew was that he desired her and it was lusty, hot sex, nothing deeper.

Despite their connection and easy conversation, she felt she had never touched Wyatt emotionally and the realization that she wanted to disturbed her.

"Was Katherine your only real love?" she asked.

He drove silently for so long, she thought maybe he hadn't heard her. Then, finally, he answered. "I met her when I was finishing law school. I was so in love with her and we got engaged. She wasn't as much in love with me, apparently, and then someone else came along. He was older, successful, a U.S. senator, and the first thing I knew, we were no longer engaged and she was out of my life forever. That's the one time I've been truly and deeply in love."

"Are you over her?"

"In a way. In another way, I don't ever want to go through that kind of pain again so I'm careful about relationships. To that extent, maybe I'm not over her."

"You have your parents, your siblings—you're not accustomed to loss."

"I've lost grandparents I loved and it hurts. I guess I was deeply in love with Katherine, actually blindly in love with her or I would have seen what was happening. What about you? Ever been deeply in love?"

"No. I had a wild crush in college for a while, but then it sort of faded away for both of us. No big hurt when we parted. We just mutually agreed our feelings for each other were over. I'd like to love a man with all my heart—but that hasn't happened yet."

"Maybe you're fortunate. Love can hurt," he said in a matter-of-fact tone.

"At least you can talk about loving your ex-fiancée. That's a good sign."

"It's getting to be a long time since law school. Time helps."

"I'll bet you've left some broken hearts in Verity and probably anywhere else you've lived."

He smiled. "Don't know much about that. I haven't been close enough to a woman to break her heart."

"So now you've given me warning to avoid falling in love with you."

He smiled again. "I don't think there's the slightest danger of that happening. You and I are both too strong-willed to fall in love, plus too much at cross-purposes over your reasons for being in Verity. We have busy lives that are poles apart in what we do and where we live. Nope—we're both safe from even the slightest heartbreak. But I'll miss you and the best sex I ever had."

She laughed. "I better not fall in love with you. Sheesh! With that description, you would never return my love. You didn't add that you won't really risk your heart again. Part of you is closed to the world."

"You've got it right."

"Wyatt, sometimes in affairs of the heart, we can't always control what we feel. I know that you intend to control everything in your life, but it doesn't always work that way."

"It will where my heart is concerned," he said in a flat voice and a chill slithered around her heart because she had never heard so much determination in one brief sentence that had been spoken quietly.

"Thank heavens I'm not head over heels in love with you, then." She said it flippantly, but couldn't quell the disturbed feeling in her stomach. "Does Katherine live in Verity or Dallas or in D.C. with the senator?"

"No. He's no longer a senator and they live in Cleveland, his hometown, where he's head of a company that is headquartered there. I wish them well. If she showed up tomorrow, divorced and wanting to go out together, I don't feel like I'd be interested. I imagine we've grown apart over time and I wouldn't trust her again. We were kids, in law school. Life is different now and we're both different. Last I heard she had two kids."

"If you're truly over her, I wouldn't think your heart would still be locked away."

"I just don't want that kind of pain." He glanced quickly at her and then back at the road. "Trust me, I'm over her. Tonight I'll be with a sexy, gorgeous redhead so I'll be blind where other women are concerned. I definitely can't wait for the rest of the evening after my family leaves."

She reached over to place her fingers lightly on his thigh and saw his chest expand as he inhaled deeply.

"Who will be at your house?"

"You've met most of them now. Nick will be there. He's the state representative and his life is politics. He's the one who lost his pregnant wife in a car wreck."

"That's really tough. It hurt terribly when we lost Dad, Mom and my grandfather."

"Sorry. Nick hides his hurt, but he keeps busy and out in the public. I think part of that is to avoid going home and being by himself."

"I can understand. When Mom died, it tore up my grandparents and it was so hard on Desirée. We'd already lost Dad. I tried to be the rock for all of them, which actually helped me sometimes. You get through it because you have no choice. I'm sorry for Nick, though. That's a dreadful loss."

"They have a bad loss in the Calhoun family, too, if you get to meet all of Lindsay's siblings. Mike Calhoun's wife died from cancer. He has a little two-year-old, Scotty. You may not meet Mike. He lives on a ranch and stays home with Scotty. He isn't over his loss and he doesn't socialize much. Mike's quiet and a loner. At least Nick gets out and mingles with people all the time and that helps."

"It does help. That's what I've always done." She could see that Wyatt was affected by Mike's loss, even though he was a Calhoun. She tried to lighten the mood by asking, "Who else will be there tonight?"

"Tony—you know him." Wyatt smiled as he talked about his brother. "He's definitely his own person and has his own ideas."

"He's delightful. You, Nick, Tony," she said. "Where does Madison fit in?"

"I'm the oldest, then Madison, Nick and Tony's the baby. Madison and Jake were high school sweethearts and our parents didn't want them to marry. Dad got wind that they were planning to elope and he stopped it. Actually, he was underhanded about it, but he thought Jake might be headstrong—which he probably would have been. They didn't know what Dad had done until this year. They're happy now and old enough to know they want to be together." He cast her a glance. "While you're here, are you going to try to meet more Calhouns?"

"Yes, if I get the chance. I liked Lindsay and Jake. They were both cooperative and friendly."

"Jake usually is. Lindsay may offer to introduce you around to the rest of her family."

They passed two metal posts with barbed-wire fences stretching away on either side. They drove long enough on a graveled road that she turned to him.

"Where is your house? How big is this ranch?"

"It's big and I'm far away from the highway. The ranch is different from my house in town. This is where I'd rather be. There is nowhere on earth as great."

"That's a true Texan. Ah, finally," she said as they topped a rise and she saw lights. It was still dusk and she could see the sprawling house and buildings beyond it.

She was amazed by the number of buildings and the size of his house and outbuildings. Judging from the smile on Wyatt's face, he felt at home here, and she was seeing yet another side to Wyatt.

Cars and pickups were parked along the wide drive at the back of the house. He parked and came around the car and as she watched him, she forgot all about dinner with his family. Tall, broad-shouldered, purposeful in his stride, Wyatt took all her attention and she wanted to be in his arms. Again, she wondered how he had captured her interest so quickly and thoroughly.

The wraparound porch was welcoming with flowers in pots and flowers still blooming in beds that flanked the porch. Tall, wooden rocking chairs were scattered on the porch along with a hammock, small tables, a couple of padded chaise lounges. The place looked inviting and comfortable.

Inside, lights blazed and her curiosity rose about Wyatt's family. They entered through a wide hallway with boots lined against the wall, a hat stand that held half a dozen wide-brimmed Western hats. Wyatt held her arm lightly while tempting smells of cooking beef and barbecue assailed her. She could see part of the kitchen through an open door and two cooks in uniforms with aprons bustled back and forth.

Going through another door with Wyatt, she entered a wider hall that ran the length of the house. Two-story-high, beamed ceilings added to the spaciousness in the big hallway that was lined with oil paintings of Western scenes.

The house revealed more of the billionaire side of Wyatt with luxurious furniture, a thick hall runner on the polished hardwood floor, crystal chandeliers and, visible through the back of the house, a fountain and a pool.

"You have a beautiful home," she said.

He gave her a crooked grin. "Thanks. It's comfortable. You've only seen the back and the hall. Sometime later we'll take a tour. I want you to see my bedroom."

"I can't wait," she said, her mouth going dry. She knew his reason for wanting her there, and while she agreed, she thought she'd learn a lot about this handsome cowboy from his private quarters. His smile had vanished and the look in his eyes held a promise of hot kisses later in the night.

"Right now you get to know my family better. They have bugged me about getting together with you since they discovered you were in Verity."

"Here I am." She had enjoyed meeting them at the hotel and now she wanted to get to know them better.

"Follow the noise and we'll find them, probably out on the patio because it's a nice evening."

Wyatt turned to pass through a large living area with a giant-screen television, a wet bar, clusters of brown leather chairs, leather sofas and tables. A huge stone fireplace filled one corner of the room. They stepped outside onto a long patio that ran the length of the back of the house. Beds of blooming flowers filled the yard.

"This is so pretty," she said, gesturing around the yard.

"Thanks. I love it out here where it's quiet. Something you probably can't understand."

"You're accustomed to that life. I need people around me and things going on. It's what I'm accustomed to, just as this has always been your life."

As they joined the others, Destiny was greeted by Madison and Jake who glowed with happiness. Jake smiled at her. "I'm happy to have this chance to get to know another Calhoun better. How distantly are we related?" he asked.

"My great-great-great-grandfather was Eldridge Calhoun. It's my mother's side of the family. Her mother was a Calhoun and her grandfather was a Calhoun. I have a family tree at home."

"I'm not familiar with Eldridge Calhoun. I'll have to look him up. So the feud has never mattered in your family?"

"No," she replied, "at least not for my mom. Now, Mimi,

my grandmother, is different. She's more into the feud. She's warned me about the Milans," she replied, smiling and Jake grinned, slipping his arm around Madison's waist.

"Someone should have warned me she was going to steal my heart," he said lightly.

"My grandmother really hasn't ever known any Milans. We moved to California when I was young and we don't know a lot of family members who live around here. My mother lost touch completely and she died rather young."

"Sorry," Jake said. "We'll have to have you out so you can meet my family and at least know this branch of the Calhouns. You already know Lindsay, so there's just Mike, his little boy, Scotty, and my other brother Josh that you haven't met. Our parents live in California now.

"I'd love to meet the other Calhouns."

She turned as Nick greeted her with an infectious smile. "I enjoyed your interview and was delighted that all was harmonious between the Milans and the Calhouns," Nick said.

Destiny nodded her thanks. "I think it was entertaining and interesting. While Lindsay said the feud was still alive, she was quite pleasant."

Nick grinned. "I think Lindsay and Tony were on their best behavior for their families' benefit."

"I'll second that one," Jake said. "I suspect she was being nice to her newlywed brother and sister-in-law."

"I was happy with the interview and the audience we had," Destiny said.

"Have you seen the Wrenville house yet?" Jake asked her.

"Oh, yes. We plan to go back again while we're here. We might look around a bit for any hidden letter or fortune. That would be quite a discovery," she said, smiling, glancing at Wyatt, who looked amused.

"Don't get your hopes too high," he cautioned. "A lot of kids have searched that house."

"I'm surprised it's not more than kids," she said.

"According to rumors and gossip," Jake stated, "Lavita Wrenville was an eccentric old maid who lived on a pittance left by her father. People are divided on opinions about Lavita Wrenville, but the majority think she started the rumors of saving her money and living a miserly existence shut up in that old house. Most people think she died penniless just as she had lived in poverty. From the time she was young until she died an old woman, there was no money coming in, only what her father left for her."

Wyatt added to the story. "According to the old-time bankers, Lavita drew the money out of the bank and kept it at the house, so no one really knows, but with it going out and no more coming in, I don't expect we'll ever find a fortune there."

"Stories abound, although they're beginning to die out because we're far enough removed from Lavita's generation that there's little interest," Nick stated.

"I find all of it rather fascinating," Destiny said. "I saw her portrait that hangs in the historical museum along with her mother's and father's portraits. It was painted when she was a young woman and she looked pretty in the painting."

"I think it's a good thing no one painted her picture in later life," Madison remarked. "From all we've heard, she didn't take care of herself or her home."

"I still think it's an intriguing story," Destiny said. She caught Wyatt looking at her intently and she let her eyes lock with his. Whatever he thought, there was no way to tell by looking at him. His expression didn't change, yet in gazing at him, she felt that flash of attraction that made her forget Lavita and everyone around her for a few seconds as she felt shut away with Wyatt.

Someone was talking and she realized they might be saying something to her. She tried to shift her attention from Wyatt, feeling a faint flush because she had lost the entire train of conversation.

She heard greetings and laughter and turned to see Tony Milan enter the room and stop to talk to one of servers who approached to take their drink orders. Tony looked like the epitome of a Texas cowboy in jeans, boots and a red Western shirt. She was certain he had hung his hat when he entered the house. She seemed to remember Wyatt once saying that Tony was a rodeo rider, and she could easily see him in that venue.

"You can always tell when Tony arrives because his enthusiasm spills over. He doesn't make a quiet, unobtrusive entrance," Wyatt remarked, greeting his brother as Tony joined them.

"Hi, Destiny," he said and she smiled at him.

"I'm glad to see you again. Thanks for adding a nice touch to the interview."

"Wouldn't have missed it for the world," he said, grinning. "Good luck in making a story out of that old Wrenville place. That all happened a long time ago."

"If it isn't interesting, it won't be a show. Right now, I'm just looking into it."

She was delighted to find out he was a fan of her show, and knowledgeable about the mysteries they'd covered. While she liked talking about them, she turned the tables on Tony. "So I hear you're the rodeo performer."

Tony grinned. "I love the challenge. It beats politics." He elbowed Nick beside him. "I keep trying to talk my brother into taking up bronc riding but he won't bite. Now, Wyatt's deal is calf roping." Tony's blue eyes twinkled as he spoke and with his good-natured ribbing of his brothers, he looked ready for fun and interested in everyone.

Nick laughed. "I can't find riding a bucking bronc quite in the same league as dealing with the laws of the land and making decisions that may help our quality of life. I like the challenges of politics, too, but I will admit they're a far cry from trying to stick on the back of a contrary horse."

"Ask Madison about her barrel racing," Tony suggested to Destiny.

Madison laughed. "That was short-lived," she said. "Too hard on the legs and my art became a lot more important. Tony is definitely our family's rodeo performer."

"To each his own," he said, smiling at Destiny. Standing close to him, she could see flecks of green in his blue eyes. Handsome and charismatic, he would be fun to have on her show if she could think of a way to work him into the program, assuming there was one.

Over drinks Destiny listened to the Milans and Jake talk about Verity and telling funny stories about the locals, and she realized Wyatt had a warm, close-knit family with compatible siblings.

She sat beside Nick, who didn't have the exuberance of his younger brother, but had his own friendly manner.

"Destiny, tell me what politicians you've had on your show or worked with in California."

"There have been quite a few." She named several. "They were cooperative, easy to work with."

"That's because they were probably looking for votes," Nick said, smiling at her. "Goes with the job."

"You didn't get interviewed for the show. How do you feel about the feud?"

"It doesn't exist for me," he answered easily. "I don't have a quarrel with any of the Calhouns. Not until one runs against me for public office," he added, drawing a smile from Destiny.

She looked at the three brothers. "All of you are so different, but then I'm different from my sister. Wyatt is the quiet one, I see."

Nick agreed. "Wyatt is our rock. Our dad was a busy lawyer and later a judge. By high school if we had problems to take to Dad, we'd take them to Wyatt instead. He's levelheaded, smart, able to work through problems. He would have been a hell of a trial lawyer, but he's a cowboy at heart. He loves his ranch and he has the resources to do what he wants. Wyatt likes a simple life. He has an island where he spends time occasionally in the cold of January or February, but otherwise, he's on his ranch if he can be."

"True," Wyatt said as he clapped his brother on the back. "Can't think of any place I'd rather be."

Destiny turned to Wyatt, looking into his blue eyes and shutting out the others. For a moment she could only think about being alone with him later in the evening.

Through a delicious barbecue dinner with platters of ribs and afterward, she enjoyed the Milans and Jake and was surprised when Tony stood to go. Glancing at her watch, she saw it was almost midnight.

Madison and Jake stood next, saying they hadn't realized the time, and Nick followed.

It was another thirty minutes before each one finished telling her goodbye and they all went out the door. She stood on the porch with Wyatt as they left.

"So now do I get my purse to go?"

"Don't even think about it. I'm just waiting until they get underway."

"What a nice family you have," she said. "You're fortunate, Wyatt."

"I know I am. They're a great family. We enjoy each other and that's good. It's good we all live here, too. I expect Nick to be in D.C. at some point, but he'll always come home. Jake is gone a lot in his energy business, so Madison will be gone with him."

"I love her art. She's very talented."

"Yes, she is."

"So you and Tony are the ones who'll be here all the time."

"Probably. There they go," he said as the last car pulled away. He draped his arm across her shoulders. "We're alone. The cook has gone to his quarters, and his staff has left for the day."

They entered the house and Wyatt locked up, switching on the alarm. She watched as he moved around.

He took her hand. "Come let me give you a tour—we'll start with my bedroom."

"I can't wait," she said breathlessly. "It was a delightful evening."

"I enjoyed it, but I was ready for them to go home about two hours ago so we could be alone."

She smiled at him as they held hands and climbed the winding stairs to the second floor.

"You looked gorgeous tonight, but that's nothing new," he said.

"It's new to hear you tell me and I love to hear that from you. I want to dazzle you, Wyatt, to break through that armor you keep around yourself. You only give so much and no more."

"I've told you why and I didn't think there was anything lacking in our relationship. Is this a complaint?"

She smiled at him and ran her fingers across his chest as they walked down a wide hall together. "I think not. Absolutely no complaints over being with you. I just want to dazzle you is all."

"Believe me, I'm dazzled. I can barely get my breath. Here's my room," he said, switching on lights as they entered a large living area with a rolltop desk, bookshelves, a big-screen television and other electronic equipment, leather sofa and chairs, another huge rock fireplace, and a built-in fish tank with exotic fish.

"This is marvelous, Wyatt," she said, turning to face him.

"You're marvelous and I'm spellbound," he said in a

husky voice as he slid his arm around her waist. "I've waited way too long for this," he said before he silenced her reply with a kiss.

Her heart thudded and she wrapped her arms around his neck, holding him tightly, wanting him more than she would have guessed possible. She, too, felt as if it had been days she had waited for this moment. She wanted to be in his arms, making love, holding him close the rest of the night. She didn't want to think about how different they were, or the way he'd closed off his heart. She didn't want to think about parting with him or Wyatt going out of her life. The realization startled her momentarily.

Was she falling in love with him?

Seven

She felt caught in a dizzying spiral as desire for Wyatt consumed her. She wanted him with her whole being and felt she couldn't get enough if they loved for hours.

She kissed him passionately, pouring out her feelings, wanting to break through that barrier he kept around his heart. Each time they loved, it was hot, sexy, but there was always a part of him that he kept to himself, a shuttered look in his eyes. As slight as it was, she could feel it as they loved and she wanted him to lose that with her, to let go and pour himself completely into loving, to stop being afraid to give of himself completely.

Clothes were a barrier and soon tossed aside. She caressed him, determined to drive him as wild as he drove her.

Later, as Wyatt kissed her, he picked her up to carry her to his bed. He trailed kisses along her throat and over her breasts, his mouth following his hands as he caressed her, over her waist, her hips, her legs, taking his time as if he cherished her. Then he reversed the trail of kisses from her feet to her neck. No man had ever done this, kissed her like this, as if every part of her was special and deserving of attention. And she reveled in it.

But the warmth he elicited was nothing compared to the fire he ignited in her when he placed her legs on his shoulders and used his hands and tongue to stir a tempest in her. She enjoyed the sensations, allowed herself to bask in them, until she hovered near release. She didn't want to find that ecstasy alone; she wanted Wyatt with her. She lowered her legs and pulled him into the V they created, a special space just for him.

When he finally entered her, she held him tightly, her long legs wrapped around him, moving with him and trying to make their loving last as long as possible.

Her head thrashed, her long red hair spilling over her shoulders in wild disarray.

Sweat beaded on Wyatt's forehead and on his broad shoulders as he tried to keep control, to love her. She felt wound tighter and tighter until she crashed into release, her hips rocking with him as his control vanished and he pumped furiously.

Pleasure poured over her and she felt him shudder with his climax. She held him as close as possible and in that moment, she felt in love for the first time in her life.

Her eyes flew open. As if he sensed something, Wyatt slowed and turned his head to kiss her. She held him tightly, kissing him, even as she felt a sense of panic because she was in love with him and it was something that couldn't be and she never intended to have happen.

In his arms she'd found rapture, satisfaction and now an added factor. Love that couldn't be stopped or avoided because it had already happened. She was in love with a tall, Texas cowboy, a rancher, a man whose heart was locked away and a man as different from her as a city sidewalk from a country lane. "I love you." She mouthed the words, but didn't even whisper them.

She loved him. She trusted him. She wanted to be with him. He brought calmness to her life she didn't have. With Wyatt, as nowhere in her busy life, she wasn't always the one in charge. In her job, hers was often the final call, and in her life, it seemed as if she'd been taking care of her family forever, her mother, her grandmother and her sister. Wyatt made her feel that the decisions didn't all have to be hers, that everything wasn't resting on her shoulders alone.

She didn't want to tell him goodbye and return to Chicago and go on with her life without ever seeing Wyatt again.

How had she let this happen?

"You're fantastic," Wyatt whispered, kissing her lightly again as his weight came down more on her. She held him tightly still, absorbing the moment, putting off separation from him. For right now, she loved him and she held him against her heart and this was a good moment. But he didn't feel what she did. Wyatt's heart was locked away and there hadn't been a change in him. For Wyatt, theirs was a lusty relationship. For her, the relationship had changed and grown deeper.

She stroked his back. "Wyatt, this is so good," she whispered. "So very good."

He rolled over, keeping her close in his embrace and then he looked into her eyes. She gazed back, wondering how much he could see of what she felt.

He kissed her gently, carefully and then looked at her again, smoothing her damp curls away from her face. "This is all I could think about. I want you in my arms, in my bed all night long and tomorrow. You don't have to go back to town, do you?"

"I don't have appointments."

"Good. I don't want to let you go."

In due time she knew he would let her go. This was not something Wyatt wanted permanently. She'd been so sure she wouldn't fall in love with him. She had never really been in love before, but she could recognize it when it happened. She loved this tall cowboy and there was no undoing what was done.

"You're fantastic, Destiny. I just can't let you go. I want to hold you close all night, love again as often as we can. You're the sexiest woman on this earth."

"Ah, Wyatt, this is good. We should be together. You don't have to let me go. We've got the rest of the night, part of tomorrow."

"Tomorrow might not be quite enough," he said.

"You'll still have to go into town tomorrow, won't you?"

"No. That's why I have deputies. Without you there, everything will be quiet and peaceful," he said, smiling at her.

She looked up at him and laughed. "I haven't upset your life or the town that much. Don't tell me you don't ever have crime or anything going on in Verity?"

"Oh, sure. Fred Baines parked by the fire hydrant last week and within the hour the J.B. Grill caught on fire. The fire truck couldn't get up to the hydrant at first until we got the car moved. The next day I had to get the Wilcoxes' cat out of their chimney and the dead bird he carried in there."

She smiled. "I still don't think I'm the biggest problem that Verity has for the sheriff."

"You're definitely the most delightful problem," he said, nuzzling her neck and making her laugh again. She stroked his smooth back, relishing touching him, feeling the solid muscles beneath her palm.

"This is good," he whispered.

"I agree. It's perfect."

"What do you plan to do after this show? Few shows run forever."

"I have ideas for more books I want to write, and some other avenues I'd like to explore. I want to get back to California. If Desirée stays happily married, that's a responsibility I won't have, but I still try to help my grandmother. Chicago is far away from my family and I'm tied down by the show. What about you? Do you plan to retire as sheriff after the Wrenville house is taken care of and go back to being a rancher for the rest of your life? Will you be a hermit on your ranch—living out your life all alone because of something someone did years ago? You seem too full of life for that."

"I'll probably marry someday. Maybe a marriage of convenience even—"

She laughed. "Wyatt, if you marry, for her, it will not be a marriage of convenience."

He grinned and propped his head on his hand to look down at her. "I should keep you around to give my ego a boost."

"I don't think your ego needs the slightest boost. You have enough self-confidence—enough to slip over into arrogance."

"Arrogance? Me? I don't think I've been accused of that before."

"Then you've been around people who did not speak out as much as I do."

"That's accurate," he said and she laughed with him. He pulled her close, hugging her tightly as he stretched beside her. He felt hard, warm and solid and she felt another pang at the thought of telling him goodbye.

How had she fallen in love with him? She should have guarded her own heart. They hadn't known each other long but she suspected she might be in love with him for a long time to come. She shivered as she thought of how cold her life would be without him in it.

He pulled away slightly to look intently at her. "Are

you cold?" he asked, grabbing a sheet to pull over them. "Maybe I need to warm you again—or we can sit in a steamy tub or have a hot shower. What's your preference?"

"With you, how could I care which it is. You pick something. This is good right now."

He pulled her close. "So we stay right here in each other's arms." After a few moments of silence, he shifted so he could see her face. "Do you plan to marry? Have a family?"

"I've raised one child and feel as if I've had a family, so it's not so urgent, but I do want a family. A family is the best part of life. Later, maybe. I really have never found the right man."

"You would disillusion a universe of men if you made that announcement public."

"I know better than to do that," she said.

"My brother Nick is green with envy over your public relations skills. He would like to hire you, but he knows he can't."

She laughed. "He never gave an indication of that. After meeting your brother, though, I don't think he needs any help with PR. He's handsome, likable and with the tragedy in his life, he'll be sympathetic to some. He's a smart man and evidently, he's had successful political campaigns already and made all sorts of contacts here and in Washington."

"You've described Nick perfectly."

"Now, Tony... I would love to have your youngest brother on my show. Actually, each of you would be interesting. In fact, if I could get the three of you to appear—"

"Forget it, lady. No way will the sheriff of Verity, Texas, appear on *Unsolved Mysteries.*"

She laughed. "I'll wager I can get Tony and Nick to appear if I ever do a show about Verity."

"I won't take that wager. Nick would love the publicity and Tony would love flirting with you."

"Maybe Lindsay Calhoun is taking the wrong approach with Tony. I can't imagine fighting with him."

"There's not a guy on this earth who would fight with you. But Lindsay can be tough. You haven't met any of the older generation of Calhouns and Milans—that's where the feud is still alive. Lindsay's mother won't speak to any of the Milans. The Judge talks to us, but he doesn't like us. My folks don't like the Calhouns. Go back and find any grandparents—that feud is still going."

"Now you tell me."

Destiny rolled Wyatt onto his back and lay on top of him, placing her hands on the bed on either side of him to raise herself slightly. Watching him, in a slow move, she rubbed her breasts lightly against his chest. His expression changed and his blue eyes darkened, desire burning in their depths.

He wound his hand in her thick hair and tugged lightly, drawing her down to kiss her. In seconds she pulled back enough to straddle him, running her fingers lightly over him and playing with him. He was aroused, ready to make love, and he placed his hands on her narrow waist and turned her over so he was above her.

"I want you now," he whispered and kissed away any answer she had.

Later Saturday morning, Destiny sent a text to Amy telling her to take a few days off and tell Duke and Virginia to do the same. Destiny wrote that she would see them Monday.

From that moment on, she tried to shut the future, even the next week, out of her thoughts. She lived for the present moment, enjoying Wyatt's company and his ranch, until

late in the evening after they had made love and she was
in his arms as they lay on their sides talking.

"Wyatt," she said, "you're not still in love with Katherine, are you? You're just afraid to risk loving again."

He stared at her for a few silent moments. "I suppose
you're right. I don't really want Katherine in my life anymore. I just never want to go through that kind of loss."

"Life doesn't come with guarantees. Sometimes it's
worth the risk."

He looked amused and one corner of his mouth lifted.
"Is this a proposal?"

"Don't be silly." She cocked her head and looked intently at him. "I'm not ready to say goodbye." She ran
her fingers in his thick hair. "I'm here, Wyatt. You better
guard that frozen, locked-away heart of yours well. I may
want to unlock it more than I want to find the secrets of
the Wrenville house."

His eyes narrowed a fraction and then his expression
changed when he gave her another faint smile. He ran his
fingers lightly over her bare shoulder. "You just want what
you can't have, Destiny. You rise to a challenge. If I'd propose to you, you'd say no and I'd probably have a difficult
time getting to see you."

"You think? Well, you haven't, so hang on. As the man
said, 'You ain't seen nothin' yet,'" she drawled in a breathy,
sultry voice. She leaned closer, tracing the curve of his ear
with the tip of her tongue, then the corner of his mouth
and then his lower lip. "Maybe it is the challenge I love.
We'll see," she whispered.

With a groan Wyatt enveloped her and he kissed her
possessively, a hard, deep kiss that ended all talk.

Hours later, she lay stretched against him, held in his
arms while he slept for the first time since they had been
together. She shifted, turning on her side to look at him,
placing her hand lightly on his chest. His arms tightened
around her, but in a short time, he relaxed and soon his
breathing was deep and even again.

She had found the thing he feared most—being hurt again. She knew that with his attitude toward love there was no permanent future for them, yet she loved him and she didn't want to pack, tell him goodbye and return to Chicago to never see him again. This was the first time love had come into her life. She was surprised, shaken and uncertain how to deal with it.

She settled against him, staring into the room that had only one soft lamp glowing. How could she have fallen in love with him?

Sunday night she was in his arms, sitting between his legs in a king-size bathtub of hot, sudsy water. "These have been decadent, wonderful days and nights, Wyatt. We've loved, danced, loved, eaten, showered and loved some more. Hasn't been much sleeping going on."

He chuckled. "We can catch up later on sleep. This is much better. A chance you might call and cancel going back tomorrow?"

"No way. We'd be the talk of the town."

"Might at that. I suspect we might already be. You've disappeared with me for the weekend and your staff is on a break. No one has missed us much—to put that correctly, no one has missed me. I hope they think I'm showing you the sights."

"Best sights ever," she said, caressing his thigh.

"I'm the one who has had the best sights," he said as he cupped her breasts in his warm, wet hands.

"It's been good, but I should go back to town tomorrow morning. You know I should have gone back tonight."

"I know no such thing. I want you here with me as long as possible."

"You're making me rethink Monday. Maybe we should let the town gossip. I'll bet they haven't had anything to gossip about you since my sister was here."

"Not even then. Everyone was so taken with the movie

as well as Desirée that they had a lot of things to talk about. Let's get out of this tub and you can text Amy and tell her you'll be back Thursday before you change your mind."

"So now it's Thursday you want. Wyatt, that's almost a whole week."

"There'll be gossip either way, so make it Thursday. We're already the number-one gossip topic in Verity."

"You'll get tired of me," she replied.

"Let me dispel that idea right now," he said, lifting her cascade of auburn hair to kiss her nape.

It was two in the morning on Thursday when he took her to her suite at the Verity Hotel and it was four in the morning before Wyatt left to drive to his Verity home and get an hour's sleep before work.

He got to the office before anyone else arrived. A little before seven Val arrived and minutes later Dwight entered.

"It's been a calm, quiet week," Val said.

"People have been getting to know the Boydens and Ms. Osgood, who is as nice as Destiny," Dwight said. "We had her out to dinner Sunday night because my wife got to know her when she talked to her at length about Destiny's first book," Dwight stated.

"The Boydens drove to Dallas. They got some tips on places to eat, things to see," Val added.

Wyatt didn't want to think about Destiny's staff and how their job here would soon be done. All too soon now she would leave for Chicago. He wasn't ready to tell her goodbye. He wanted her to stay a lot longer. "I'll go see what's on my desk," Wyatt said, turning to leave.

"Duke Boyden said they will go out to the Wrenville house today and spend the day. He didn't say, but I think they're going to look for the legendary letter that Lavita is supposed to have written," Dwight said.

"I wish them lots of luck," Wyatt remarked dryly. "I

don't think any such letter exists. I can't imagine that Lavita Wrenville had a fortune to hide or any big secret she actually intended to pass along. Kids have hunted through that house in years past over and over and never found anything."

"Are you going to try to stop her from looking?" Val asked.

"No. Let them look. It won't hurt, as long as they don't disturb the structure of the house. When it reverts to Verity next year, we'll go through it carefully first and tear it down, but that's different."

Wyatt headed to his office, leaving the door open as he sat behind his desk. There was no way he could stop her search, but at least she was bringing an air of excitement and fun to everyone so far. He might as well resign himself to acceptance. She'd won this round.

He received a text and pulled out his phone to read it.

Miss you. Going to W. house later if you want to join us. Will look around for the letter.

See you this pm. Plan on dinner with me, he replied. He wanted to see her and he missed her when he got to his house from the hotel in the early hours. For certain he wanted her in his arms when he went to bed tonight.

If he could, he would go to the hotel now and make love to her this morning, but he didn't think she would cooperate and he knew he had work to do. Nothing earthshaking though, but he would really stir gossip if he took more days off. He smiled, thinking she had set his world spinning a different direction. Nothing had been the same since he had spotted the red limo in his parking spot. It had been a red flag warning of change in his quiet life.

He thought about her going back to Chicago. Even though they hadn't talked about it, he knew it would be soon. He was going to miss her. That realization still shocked him. He never missed the women who went out of his life—at least, not since Katherine.

He thought about Destiny's warning that she wasn't ready to say goodbye. He was certain that simply was because if he had proposed or begged her to stay longer, he thought she would pack and go, turn down his proposal and be on her way without a qualm. She was accustomed to getting her way and having things under control in her life and that was what the warning to him had been about. They weren't in love.

The moment he declared that to himself, he frowned. What did he feel for her? He didn't want her to go back yet. Later, it would be okay, but right now she was a fantastic lover and he wanted her with him in his bed for a lot more nights before they said goodbye. He liked the long talks they had, the fun, the silly moments, just being with her and looking at her, holding her soft warmth close in his arms. She was one person he could talk freely to about whatever he wanted. She always seemed interested and was a good listener, even more so than Katherine had been. He wanted to keep her in his life a lot longer.

It was a good thing he hadn't fallen in love with her. She wouldn't return the emotion and she would be gone in a flash. He couldn't imagine Destiny settling on a ranch in obscurity. She was meant for the life she had—out in public, in the limelight, playing to an audience. He wasn't in love, but he wanted to be with her right now, tonight, and he didn't want her to go back to Chicago anytime in the near future.

His phone rang and he saw it was Dwight.

"Wyatt, Duke Boyden is here. He wants to see you."

"Send him back," Wyatt said, hanging up and standing to walk to the door. As soon as Duke came in sight, Wyatt smiled. Dressed in his black chauffeur's uniform that pulled across his thick shoulders, Duke approached him with a swing of his shoulders in a take-charge walk that was masculine and proclaimed control. In seconds, Wyatt offered his hand to receive a tight grip.

"Come in. Have a seat."

"Sure," Duke said, following Wyatt into his office and closing the door.

Figuring Destiny had sent Duke to ask him something about the Wrenville house, Wyatt sat in the other wing-back chair facing Duke.

"Sheriff, I don't want you to take offense, but I thought we should talk."

Startled, Wyatt focused more intently on Duke. "Sure. Go ahead."

"Virginia and I have known Amy and Destiny a long, long time. They're both like sisters to me."

Forgetting the Wrenville place, Wyatt waited in silence.

"I just want to try to avoid seeing Destiny get hurt."

Wyatt had to bite back a laugh. The moment was too ridiculous for him to get angry. "How's that?"

"It's just that she's never been interested, really interested in any of the men she meets. I think she might be in you. She doesn't usually get very involved with any of them. I don't want to see her unhappy."

"I think you made this clear before. And I think you're being influenced by Desirée."

"No, not at all. Desirée wants nearly every man she meets and she's on an emotional roller coaster over them."

"I still feel that there might be a threat in this conversation."

"Oh, no, not at all," Duke said blandly. "I'm just looking out for Destiny."

"She's a grown woman."

"I know, but she's still vulnerable. People are in matters of the heart."

"I think I can put your mind at ease. There is no matter of the heart here."

"Actually, she just spent a week with you. Destiny doesn't do things like that."

They stared at each other and Wyatt knew he had just been threatened and that Duke felt Destiny was in love, which was not the situation. They were deeply involved in hot sex, nothing more.

"Do you always talk to the men who take her out?"

Duke stared at him for a few seconds before shaking his head. "This is a first. There's never been a need before and I've known her and chauffeured her since her mother was alive."

Wyatt was silent. Now he was puzzled and his curiosity had deepened.

Duke stood so Wyatt came to his feet. "I've got to get back. She wouldn't be happy if she knew I was here, because she feels she can take care of herself. She's a caring woman. She's taken care of her parents, her sister, her grandparents, Amy. Destiny is a caring person and I don't want her hurt."

"She won't be unless it's because she doesn't find anything at the Wrenville house," Wyatt said and Duke gave him a hard look.

"Maybe we'll see you out there. Don't come to the door. I know my way out," Duke said and left, leaving the door open behind him.

Wyatt shook his head. The man was part bodyguard, part pit bull and all protector. Problem was Duke had threatened him and there was a law against threatening an officer of the law, but Wyatt wouldn't pursue it and Duke knew that he wouldn't.

According to Duke, that was the first time he'd ever talked to a man about his relationship with Destiny and he had known her for years—maybe since she was a teen.

That meant Duke thought she was more serious now than ever in her past. Did he think she was in love?

That thought shook him slightly, but Wyatt felt Duke was wrong about how serious his relationship was with Destiny.

Wyatt went back to his desk, trying to go through the mail. After thirty minutes, he shoved aside the stack of letters. He had read three, but his thoughts kept jumping back to Destiny. Twice he had reached for the phone to call her.

Wyatt slammed shut his desk drawer, got up and took his hat off the rack to jam it on his head. He walked down the hall in long strides.

When Dwight looked up, Wyatt nodded. "I'm going to the Wrenville house to see what Destiny and her staff are doing."

"Sure," Dwight said, his eyes getting wider. "She's going to be disappointed. No one thinks there is anything in that house. Not a fortune—not even a little money and no letter revealing which man shot the other."

"I agree, but she doesn't live here, so she has high hopes."

"Too bad. At least it's a pretty day."

"Sure is. I'll be back later." Clamping his jaw closed, Wyatt left the building and headed for his car. He made a U-turn and headed east for the Wrenville house. His pulse quickened and all he could think about was being with Destiny in a short time.

How disappointed would she be when she didn't find anything at the house? He figured she had been through things like this before and she would simply pack and go back to Chicago and move on to her next project. Each time he thought about her going home, the idea of life without her disturbed him more than it had before.

Eight

Destiny and Amy took the front half of the house while the Boydens took the back half to search for any hidden objects. Her pulse jumped and excitement sizzled through her bloodstream like an electrical current. But it wasn't the anticipation of finding a fortune or solving the mystery of this house that had her so excited. It was Wyatt. Tonight she would be going out with him again, and she could hardly wait. He was the talk of the town now, but it was his town and his decision to see her. He knew what he wanted to do.

She stood in the spacious front bedroom. Sunlight spilled through the wide windows that would have allowed breezes to cool the room in warm weather. She ran her hands over the walls, while Amy followed, tapping lightly with a small hammer to see if she could discover any hollow places. At one point, Destiny stood in the center of the room, studying it slowly and carefully, looking for anything out of the ordinary. She heard the car first and then

Amy glanced out the window. "It's the sheriff's car," she said, which Destiny had already guessed.

"He'll find us up here. We don't have to go down to the door," Destiny said, continuing to look around.

"You're going out with him tonight?"

"Yes, I am. He's taking me to dinner."

"We'll tell him goodbye soon."

"I know." Her gaze swept the room. "I hope I'm coming back to film this place. I would really like to find something."

"Me, too. Otherwise, it's an intriguing puzzle, but I don't know if it would be enough for a show."

"If Lavita Wrenville was old and sick and wrote the letter and hid what money she had left toward the end of her life, I think it would be in this bedroom, which I assume would have been hers if she had lived here alone."

"That makes sense. Or she could have stayed in the room she grew up in and hidden something there."

"We'll search the entire house, but I just want to go over this room extra carefully."

"Anybody home?"

"We're upstairs, Wyatt," Destiny replied and in seconds she heard his boots and the creaking boards as he climbed the stairs.

"How's the search?" he asked, stopping in the doorway and pushing his brown hat back on his head. She gazed at him, wanting to cross the room and kiss him, wanting his arms around her and knowing neither would happen because they weren't alone.

"I'm sure you won't be surprised—we haven't found anything."

He greeted Amy then asked, "Where are Duke and Virginia?"

"They're taking the back side of the house while we're going through the front," Destiny answered.

Wyatt looked around. "In less than a year, we'll officially search this place in a thorough hunt that will include tearing out walls and floorboards inside the house. You can come back and film then."

"Thanks for that offer," she replied. "I'll keep it in mind. In the meantime, we plan to continue this search. Have you ever heard which bedroom Lavita had?"

"No. I don't know any details other than what I've already told you."

She continued to move slowly around the room, tapping the walls, aware of Wyatt standing with his arms folded, watching the proceedings. After a while he left the room and she heard him go downstairs and outside.

Finally she had to admit they had come up empty. "Amy, I give up here. Let's move on."

"I agree. I don't think anything is hidden here."

As she passed the window, she saw Wyatt standing by his car while he talked on his phone.

As they searched another room, he returned, apparently just ending his conversation. "I'll be back at the office in a little while, once one of my deputies relieves me out here."

"You're waiting to see if we find something," Destiny said when he ended the call. "You don't have to worry. I'll tell you if we do."

He nodded. "I know, but the town has a vested interest and no doubt someone will ask if we checked to see if you found anything. I'm sure people know you're looking."

She laughed. "You want to make sure we don't find the treasure and take it back to Chicago."

"I don't really think there's much danger of that happening, but I'm going to have to answer questions."

"As long as you're just standing there, you ought to help search," Destiny teased, looking at him and feeling that flare of desire that she always did with Wyatt.

"Our turn will come and until then, I'm happy just to watch."

Destiny concentrated on looking, but she couldn't forget Wyatt behind her, standing nearby.

When they were finished with the upstairs, she and Amy moved to the attic next and Wyatt followed. The attic hadn't been cleaned for her arrival and was filled with cobwebs and dust. Most of it had been floored, which should make their search easier and she didn't have to worry about one of them falling.

When Duke and Virginia came up, Duke set up powerful flashlights that lit up a good portion of the attic.

"We can start here and work our way around," he said. "Why don't we all four search up here and get through and out of this dust?"

Destiny agreed.

Wyatt sat on a pile of boards that had been left years earlier. "In the winter there are probably rats and mice that take shelter in here, but it's still too warm for them to come in yet."

"I don't want to think about that," Destiny said. She assigned areas to each person and she took a far corner. She ran her hands lightly along some of the boards, but some had splinters sticking out and she avoided them. In the corner, she got down on her knees and crawled into a narrow space where the light was dimmer. Looking beside a long rafter that ran to the floor, she saw short boards had been clumsily nailed in the corner beside the rafter.

"Find something interesting in those old boards?" Wyatt asked. She glanced around to just see the lower part of his legs. He leaned down to look at her. "Is there something down here?"

"I don't know. Someone has nailed some boards back here. It's a sloppy job. Get a hammer from Duke and let me see if I can take this apart."

In seconds Wyatt was back and bent down again with a hammer in hand. "If you'll come out of there, I'll do whatever you want."

"You can't fold up enough to get in this corner. Let me have the hammer."

He handed it to her and she worked, trying to pry out nails, letting them fall on the attic flooring. Finally a board hung by one nail and she peered behind it.

"Wyatt, can I have a flashlight?"

When he handed her a flashlight, she aimed it at the space she had revealed. "Here's a box," she said, working to get the last nail out of the board.

"Don't tell me you've found something after all these years."

"This isn't a fun place to be. My knees are beginning to hurt." The board snapped away in her hands. She laid it on the floor and held out the flashlight. "Hold this, please."

Wyatt hunkered down and peered into the dark corner, trying to shine the light on the space she had found. "I'll be damned. You have found something."

She tugged on a metal box that filled the space. Wyatt reached past her to grasp it with one hand so they both could try to work it free. Finally, together, they got it out.

"Can you take the box, Wyatt? It's heavy. I have to get out of here and stand up."

He held a dust-covered metal box and stepped back, reaching down to help her up when she crawled out. As she did, everyone gathered around.

"I need to go back. There are some jars that were behind the box," she said.

"I can get down there to get them," Duke said.

Destiny shook her head. "I think you're too big."

"We'll see," he said. "All of you will have to get back."

Destiny picked up the box to set it on the pile of boards. She sat beside it while Amy and Virginia gathered around.

Wyatt got down to help Duke, who had scooted into the corner space. In moments he handed two sealed glass jars to Wyatt and a leather bag with a drawstring drawn tight and knotted at the top.

"Let's get all this out and take it downstairs to look at it," Wyatt said.

"That's fine," Destiny agreed, looking at everyone who worked for her. "I've had enough of this dust."

They climbed down, all brushing off dust. Wyatt combed a cobweb from her hair with his fingers while she brushed herself off.

"It's just the five of us," Destiny said, looking one by one at the group as they assembled in the front room. "I agreed and promised the governor that if we find any money, it's to go to the town of Verity."

They all looked at the glass jars Wyatt carried that held silver and gold coins. Duke carried the box and the leather bag.

"I think this is all money. It's heavy," Duke said.

"The jars hold silver dollars and coins that we can see. The box is heavy as if it's filled with money. Let's open the box and the leather bag and see what we have," Destiny said.

"The money is here," she said, touching one of the jars in which they could see the silver and gold coins. "The letter will be with this. I'm just sure."

Destiny looked down at the items they'd found, feeling a familiar thrill cascade over her body. She reached out to hug Amy and next Virginia and then Duke. "Thank you so much for taking on this job," she told them. "It's exciting to make these discoveries. We've done it before and now here again, and each time is the most thrilling ever. Let's look and see what we've found."

They all sat on the floor beside the box as she tried to open it. Wyatt reached out to help and the lid finally came

off, revealing a piece of folded leather on the top. Destiny
carefully removed it and beneath were silver and gold dollars. "There are coins," she said, "which go to the town.
Let's see what this is."

Destiny unfolded the piece of leather with great care.
Inside was a yellowed, wrinkled, folded sheet of paper.
She held her breath as she scanned the opening words.
She had found what she was looking for. She looked up to
meet Wyatt's steady gaze and she wondered what he was
thinking. Was he happy or disappointed? She couldn't tell.

"This stays between us for now," she said. "Listen…"
She read it aloud.

"'I must finally reveal the truth of the deaths in this
house. I am the last one alive who was involved that terrible night. The year had been the happiest of my life. Two
men, Mr. Reuben Calhoun and Mr. Mortimer Milan, had
asked Papa for my hand in marriage. To my deepest sor-
row, Papa had someone else in mind for my future husband, Mr. Jerome Grayson. I fear I much preferred either
Mr. Calhoun or Mr. Milan. My preference would have
been Mr. Reuben Calhoun, but I had little choice where
Papa was concerned.

"Mr. Calhoun and Mr. Milan both came to call on
the same Saturday night. Their talk became heated and
I feared they approached a fight. Papa heard them and
joined them, telling them to each leave our house and land
and not to return.

"The three men became more agitated and then pistols were drawn. I felt faint, but wanted to get help to stop
what I feared was about to happen. I ran for our stable
keeper, Leon Haymes, who had to get his pistol and then
came behind me. When I was almost to the porch steps,
I heard three shots.

"I dreaded what I would find and it was as terrible as
I expected. Mr. Calhoun was not conscious and bleeding

profusely. Mr. Milan was barely alive, but he drew my head close to whisper to me. Papa was no longer alive, but before he died, according to Mr. Milan, Papa had announced he did not want me to marry either of them. Mr. Milan told me that Papa fired at Mr. Calhoun and then turned his pistol and fired at Mr. Milan. Mr. Calhoun was not dead and he fired at Papa. Mr. Calhoun killed Papa with his shot. Mr. Milan died in my arms and by this time Leon was with Mr. Calhoun, who was never conscious and who died last. I could not go through talking about this to townspeople or officials. I did not want to bring shame to Papa or the Calhoun or Milan families, so I said they all died without revealing what happened. This is a true account of that night as told to me by Mr. Milan. Lavita Wrenville, October 12, 1891.'"

Destiny looked around. "Lavita's father shot the Calhoun and the Milan. I think we have a show."

Wyatt smiled at her as she looked at him and she still wondered what he really thought.

"This doesn't have to be made public yet," Destiny stated, staring at Wyatt.

"If the money goes into the bank, several people will know. I can talk to Horace Pringle and he'll take care of the matter and it won't make the news."

"I want to keep the letter and the governor gave me permission to use it for the show if I return it intact to Verity. I'll give you a copy."

"Why don't you take the copy and put the original in the bank until it's time for the show?" Wyatt asked.

"I'll think that over and talk to people at the station and see what they want. We might as well go back to town and regroup." She pointed to the leather bag, which was on the floor in front of Duke.

"Duke, let's see what's in the bag. Open it and we'll find out."

Excitement made her tense with anticipation. Money
and a letter. She would have a great show and this would
go into her book.

Duke untied the drawstring, opened the bag and reached
in to withdraw another handful of coins and bills. "More
money."

Virginia and Amy clapped with enthusiasm.

"I think this calls for a celebration," Wyatt said. "I'm
not part of your group, but why don't all of you come to
my house tonight? I'll have dinner and you can celebrate
your discovery. You've found what a lot of people for a lot
of years have searched for."

Destiny looked at the others. "I think it would be fun
to take Wyatt up on his offer and to celebrate a little. How
about it?"

"That's great," Amy replied.

Duke smiled, glancing at Virginia, who nodded. "We
think that will be fun," Virginia replied.

"It's time for a celebration," Duke added.

"It's up to the four of you," Wyatt said, "and I know you
want this kept quiet until you decide how to break the news
to the best advantage for your show, but I'd like to invite
my family, who knows how to keep secrets, and also my
deputies and Dwight. They're all accustomed to keeping
silent about what they know is official. It would make a
party, but inviting others will be up to you."

"If we're doing that," Destiny said, "what about the
bank president?"

"Good idea," Wyatt said, smiling at her. "That's a lot
of people, but I can vouch for each one of them keeping
this find out of the news."

"Actually, it keeps growing. Jake, your brother-in-law is
a Calhoun. I'm a Calhoun," Destiny said. "Would the other
Calhouns in Jake's family keep quiet about it?"

Wyatt thought about Jake. "I think they would. I'll ask

Jake because he'll know. Okay, party it is. I'll send a text to my cook to give him as much time as possible and I'll give you my address to put in your GPS."

Destiny wanted to celebrate and she wanted to be with Wyatt. Excitement rocked her. "Wyatt, it would be fun to read the letter tonight when we're all gathered together."

He smiled. "It will be your party. Do what you want. I'll call Horace before we head back to town," Wyatt said. "He'll take care of depositing the money so the least number of people know about it."

"I'll put the money in your car," Duke said, carrying the box and leather bag and taking keys from Wyatt, who was on his phone. Virginia and Amy followed Duke with the two jars.

Destiny waited as Wyatt continued to make calls, finally putting away his phone. "We're set. Jake is calling his family. Everyone understands that this is to be kept quiet. Once I get back to the office I should let the governor know," he said to Destiny, "since you contacted him about searching the house."

She nodded. "I'll get in touch with him, too."

"Horace Pringle will meet us at the back door of the bank and take care of the money. He'll also make a copy of the letter. I'll head back to town now. Destiny, do you want to go with me since I have the money?" Wyatt asked.

"Yes."

Duke reentered just then. "We're loaded up. The money and the letter are in your car, Sheriff."

Wyatt thanked him. "Duke, I've sent my address to your cell and you can put it in your GPS. I'll notify the gatekeeper you're all coming." He looked at Destiny. "Ready to go?"

They all left, locking the door, which seemed ridiculous to Destiny since windows were broken and the house stood vacant. Excitement hummed like a steady current and she was ready for a party and a celebration. Best of all, Wyatt had seemed to accept her finding the letter and the money and was helping them celebrate, so maybe she hadn't upset his life or his town too badly. It occurred to her, it might be her own life that received the upset if she couldn't get over her love for Wyatt.

Each minute with him just convinced her more that she had fallen in love with him, and this party and his quiet acceptance of her achievement was adding to her growing love for him.

As they drove away from the house, Wyatt took her hand. "Congratulations, you did it."

"Thank you. I'm so excited. I know this isn't what you wanted to have happen, but it's great as possible material for a show and it definitely will be material for my book."

"The news will be big until it's replaced by something else. Verity will go right along," he said.

"You've certainly mellowed about it."

"I can't fight you. You had the governor's permission. Besides, you've brought excitement and fun to Verity—and, I'll have to admit, maybe into my quiet life."

She laughed and squeezed his hand. "I could say the same back to you."

Flashing her a quick grin, he turned his attention back to the road. "You found the letter and the money, which I didn't think existed. I'll tell you what I really want. Let me pick you up tonight so you can stay at my place and I'll take you home tomorrow."

"Or take me home tonight and come in for a long nightcap," she said, placing her hand on his knee. "I'm excited, Wyatt."

"I am, too, just for a different reason."

She stroked his thigh lightly. "Not altogether a different reason," she said in a breathy voice, letting her fingers trail up the inside of his thigh.

"Maybe you should wait on that. I'd hate to explain why I drove off into a ditch in the official sheriff's car."

She laughed softly. "I'll take a rain check. It's nice of you to have us all for a party. It's short notice for your cook."

"Lawrence will rise to the occasion. He always does, and he can get additional people to help him tonight. He has a list."

Wyatt scanned his mirrors and then shot her a glance. "I'll pick you up at half past six so we will definitely be there when everyone else arrives. At the hotel, you can make another of your grand appearances. Or go out the side door and avoid the reporters. By the way, since this is short notice, I said it would be casual tonight."

"That's fine. I can do casual. Maybe you're right this time about avoiding reporters."

As they drove back to town, Destiny thought of the party that was to come, and then her time alone with Wyatt. Two or three more nights with him and then she would say goodbye. Would it really be goodbye? The realization put a damper on her excitement over her discovery. She shook away the dread of something she didn't know for certain and caressed his thigh, feeling his warmth through the thick cotton of his uniform.

"Do you really think that many people will keep this quiet?" she asked him.

"Yes, I do. I know my family can and Jake said his would. My deputies and Dwight will and Horace Pringle definitely will. I don't think there will be any problem."

"I'm amazed, but okay. I'd like to read the letter again tonight so all present can hear. They're all involved in small ways and not so small."

"Go ahead."

"It won't be the end of the world if word gets out," she reasoned. "By the time it's passed around, news of the find

will be all garbled anyway. Next year's coming quick, so
if the show is produced, it'll be timely."

It was another hour before they finished at the bank
and Wyatt accompanied her to the door of her hotel suite.
"I have the copy of the letter with me and I'll bring it tonight," she told him. "If we do the show, I'll want the original back just for the show."

"You found it. When this is all settled, it's probably
yours, although I'm sure the Verity Historical Museum
would appreciate a copy."

"They can have the real thing then." She opened her
door. "I'd invite you in, but I am covered in dust."

"I can help you shower."

Laughing, she shook her head. "This time I need to
scrub."

"I'll pick you up at six-thirty. Sure you don't want another grand exit when I pick you up?"

"No, I'll slip out the side."

"Then I'll come up and get you. See you then." He
pulled her inside quickly, taking her into his arms and
leaning over to kiss her.

"Now you'll be covered in dust," she said when he released her.

"It was worth it," he said and left.

She closed her door and put the copy of the letter on a
table in her entryway. Excitement still danced in her, but
part of it was because she was going out with Wyatt tonight and they would either both stay at his place or both
stay in her suite.

How was she going to tell him goodbye?

She didn't want to think about that moment. The evening was ahead of her and she had no intention of adding
a sour note.

She hurried to get ready.

At six-thirty she heard the light tap on her door and

opened it to face Wyatt, whose appreciative gaze went from her head to her feet in a look that made her toes curl. Her insides heated as she gazed at him. In a dark blue shirt, black slacks, black boots and a black wide-brimmed hat, he made her want to forgo the party and be alone with him for the entire evening.

"You're gorgeous, Destiny," he said in a hoarse voice, his gaze going over her red silk blouse and matching slacks with matching high heels again.

"Thank you. I'm ready," she said.

"I'm ready for you," he whispered. "What I'd like to do is carry you off to bed."

"I'd like that, too, but we can't. Too many people are waiting and the party is at your house so you have to go."

"Aw, gee whiz," he joked and she smiled.

He took her hand and they went to his car, which was parked by the side door.

"Now I get to see your Verity house," she said.

"I like it, though I like the ranch better. You may view it as the end of the world and almost totally isolated."

"If it's yours, Wyatt, I'll love it."

A little while later she was impressed when he pulled into an exclusive community. He waved at the gatekeeper as they drove through the open black iron gates and wound up a long drive to an impressive house with lights blazing.

Before she could get out, Wyatt stopped her. "It's our last night together, Destiny. I want to send everyone home early."

A sharp pain tore at her heart. *Last night together...* What did that mean to Wyatt? Did he really care or had this all been pure sex and nothing the slightest bit deeper? She had not penetrated that armor around his heart and now their affair was over. Did he care in the least?

Nine

Wyatt took her arm as they went up the steps to a wide porch with two-story Ionic columns. He opened the door and Destiny stood in a large circular entryway with an enormous crystal chandelier hanging over a round, ornate table. "Very pretty, Wyatt."

"I'll show you where you can put your purse," he said, taking her arm and walking into a wide hall to go through the first door to his right.

They entered a formal living area with a fireplace, silk-damask-covered chairs and heavy, ornate furniture that was not at all what she had envisioned would be in Wyatt's home. He closed the door and wrapped her in his arms to kiss her.

When she finally leaned away, she gazed up at him. "I think the others will be here soon."

"C'mon. You can leave your purse in here if you want. We'll gather on the patio because it's a nice night or inside in the great room."

She walked along the wide hall that opened into a large room with glass along one wall, giving a view of the pool, gardens with blooming flowers, fountains and a patio with an outdoor living area and kitchen.

"You have a beautiful home."

"Thank you. Ah, here are our first guests," he said, greeting Jake and Madison.

As people began to arrive, waiters passed drinks. Destiny was warmly greeted by Lindsay Calhoun, who introduced Destiny to her brothers, Josh and Mike.

"None of you look alike, especially Lindsay with her blond hair," Destiny said, looking at Mike's curly black hair and Josh with straight brown hair.

Josh laughed. "She's the odd one, our blondie. She doesn't even have our brown eyes either," he said. "We can't wait to hear the letter and find out who shot who."

"I'm guessing a Milan shot a Calhoun," Mike said, smiling at her. "I can't guess who shot Mr. Wrenville."

Destiny smiled. "It's interesting and I'm so excited over our discovery."

"Wyatt said you crawled back in a corner of the attic and found it. He's probably miffed because he's looked for it before," Josh said.

"We'll read it as soon as all the guests are here."

Josh was unrelenting. "All the Calhouns figure a Milan did the shooting and all the Milans probably think a Calhoun did the shooting. We figure whoever it was, he shot Lavita's father because he wouldn't give his approval for the wedding."

Destiny kept her smile. "I'm not going to spoil your surprise by telling you."

Jake and Madison joined them. "That letter better be read soon or there will be betting on who fired the fatal shots," Jake said.

Destiny couldn't help but laugh, though there was one

thing that she, too, was wondering about. "Lavita had two men who wanted to marry her. After the shooting, she never married. Why? She was one of the wealthiest young women in the town—probably in the county or in the West even. Did no one else ever want to marry her or did she grieve all her life for a lost love?"

"I suppose we do have an interesting town," Madison remarked.

Wyatt stepped up beside Destiny. "Let me have one guess what the topic of this conversation is," he said and the others laughed.

"Probably the same as every other group at this party," Mike said, shaking hands with Wyatt. "Thanks for having this tonight and inviting all of us. You had short notice."

"Lawrence is always ready to cook. I'm glad everyone could come. Josh, I'm glad you were in town. We caught our hotel mogul in a rare moment of coming home."

"Thanks, Wyatt," Josh said, shaking hands with him. "This sounds like an interesting night. I'm glad to be here."

"I guess by now Lindsay has made introductions all the way around." Destiny nodded and Wyatt continued. "Destiny, my deputy Val just arrived and I think we're all here, so this is the big moment." He looked at Destiny. "Are you ready?"

"Of course," she said, smiling at him. As she looked into his blue eyes, she was caught in a look of such longing that, momentarily, she forgot the others and the reason they were here. Her heartbeat quickened. In that moment she would have traded everything—her show, her books, her discovery—to have Wyatt's love. Startled, she tried to focus on where she was and what was happening.

"Folks—" Wyatt said in a voice that carried, but wasn't loud. Destiny wasn't surprised though when everyone became silent. "If all of you will find a seat, our Chicago celebrity, Destiny Jones, will read Lavita Wrenville's letter. I think everyone here now has met Destiny, so I don't think she needs an introduction, but we can all welcome her—Destiny Jones."

Wyatt stepped back and smiled at her and Destiny took a folded copy of the letter from her pocket.

"I'm delighted to be here and either meet you or get to know you better. You've welcomed me and my staff and made us feel at home in Verity. Today was exciting and I know you want to hear this letter and learn what happened that fateful night at the Wrenville house, especially all the Milans and the Calhouns."

She unfolded the letter and read it. The only other sound as she read was the splashing of the fountains in the gardens and the pool. When she finished, she looked up. "There you have the truth of what happened."

There was applause and conversation started again. "So a Milan didn't shoot a Calhoun and a Calhoun didn't shoot a Milan. Old man Wrenville did them both in," Josh said, shaking his head.

"I don't know the family named, the man that Lavita's father wanted her to marry," Mike added.

Josh and Mike looked at each other and then at Wyatt and all shook their heads. "No Graysons around here. Probably some older man Mr. Wrenville did business with and Lavita didn't want to marry him," Mike said.

"So you'll do a television show about this?" Josh asked her.

"I have to take all this back to my producer. But it looks a lot more likely now that we've found the letter and have a story to tell," Destiny answered. As she talked, she looked at Wyatt and for a second almost lost her train of thought. She wondered whether he would go back to the hotel with her or she would stay here with him tonight.

After a few moments, she moved on, going from clus-

ter to cluster of guests to talk to each one. It amused her
to see that Wyatt and Nick were doing the same.

Dinner was buffet style and tables had been set up on
the patio that was large enough to easily hold them.

It was almost eleven before guests began to say good-
night.

As Destiny's staff was leaving, Amy stopped beside
her. "Duke is taking us back to the hotel. I'm assuming
Wyatt will bring you?"

"Yes, he will. I'll see you tomorrow. We can fly out of
here then." As she said the words she had a hollow feeling. Flying home—away from Wyatt. How much would
it hurt to tell him goodbye?

She suspected the real hurt was going to come when
she was in Chicago and not seeing him again.

She told Duke and Virginia she would see them in the
morning.

Finally she faced Wyatt and they were the only two in
the hallway as the last of the Milans left.

"What about Lawrence and his help?"

"They left hours ago and when you read the letter I told
Lawrence to keep them all in the kitchen, so they never
heard the letter and don't know anything about it except
Lawrence. I told him we found the letter and he'd hear
about it later."

"Then you should tell him, too."

"I really don't think Lawrence cares." He took her in
his arms. "What I care about is now and you. We have this
house to ourselves and we are wasting time."

"I'm leaving for Chicago tomorrow, so I'll have to get
back to the hotel in the morning."

"Cancel the flight and I'll fly all of you home a day later
or two days later or whatever you want."

Her heart jumped because his offer meant he wanted
her to stay longer. What was the depth of his feelings for

her? Was there a crack in that barrier around his heart? "You don't mind?"

"Wouldn't have asked if I didn't want to."

"All right. Let me send a text to Amy and she can break the news."

"Make it a short text," he said, shedding his shirt.

She drew a deep breath. "How do you expect me to concentrate on a text while you're stripping in front of me?" she asked, dropping her phone on a table and walking over to wrap her arms around him and stand on tiptoe to kiss him.

She didn't know how long they kissed when he stopped her. "You send a text so they won't be looking for you in the morning and then we'll continue."

She tried to avoid looking at him as she sent the text and got an immediate "Okay" in return. "Now, that's done. I have other things to do," she said and began to unfasten his belt.

He drew her into his embrace and kissed her, and all her worries over parting temporarily vanished.

They made love all through Friday and into Saturday morning. Sunshine streamed in the window and Destiny sat up. "Wyatt, they're ready to go back to Chicago. I've stayed an extra day and I told them we would go back today."

"You mean it, don't you?"

"Yes," she said, hurting because they were going to part now and he was going to let her walk out of his life and he wouldn't look back.

She wrapped her arms around him and kissed him furiously, wanting to consume him, love him until he couldn't get along without her, just as she couldn't get along without him.

They made love again, so it was an hour later when she

once again sat up and told him she needed to get back to the
hotel. Stepping out of bed, she headed to a shower. When
she emerged, she was dressed in her red slacks and shirt.

"Now I have to go back to the hotel."

"Come eat breakfast and then we'll go."

She nibbled a few bites of toast and drank a small glass
of orange juice, but that was all she could get down.

They were quiet as he drove her to the hotel. At her door
when she faced him they looked into each other's eyes.
She could hardly believe the hurt she felt. It threatened to
crush her heart. She wanted Wyatt to want her in his life.
She didn't know how they would mesh their very different
lives, but she would find a way if only Wyatt loved her as
much as she loved him.

He stepped inside, closing the door behind him as he
kissed her.

Finally she stopped him. "I have to go, Wyatt. They're
just waiting for me to go home."

"All right. I'll talk to Duke and get someone to turn in
the limo after you go to the Verity airport. They'll take
you to my plane." He gave her one last lingering kiss. "I
may see you soon, Destiny. I'll call you," he said.

Hurting, she nodded because she didn't think he would
call or that she would see him—unless she returned to
Verity on business.

He turned and was gone, the suite door closing behind
him. She hurt all over and she trembled, feeling chilled.
She had to pull herself together because she didn't want
the others to see her this upset. It would be obvious it was
over Wyatt.

She rinsed her face in cold water, then she changed
and tossed her clothes into her bag so she would not keep
them waiting.

Two hours later, she sat quietly in Wyatt's luxurious

private jet as they gained altitude and Texas disappeared below. What was Wyatt doing? Did he hurt at all or did he even care?

Wyatt tried to work and couldn't concentrate. He gave up and told Dwight he needed to go to his ranch and would see him Monday.

As he sped along the highway, a plane went overhead. He looked up, knowing it was a commercial jet and not his plane flying Destiny home to Chicago. Even though their parting had been inevitable from the first, it hurt. He missed her and wanted her with him tonight and the rest of the week.

He would get over her. He always did, but he couldn't recall ever missing someone this badly. Was it purely the sex that had wrapped around him and ensnared him? At some point, he knew, that ardor would cool, although at the present moment, he couldn't imagine it cooling even one degree. Common sense said it would and then how would he feel about her?

He missed her, her laughter, her smiles, her surprises, her flirting, the constant excitement she stirred. Without her, the whole town of Verity seemed empty and devoid of life.

He'd give himself a few days and then he would probably be back to normal with his life back in a regular routine that did not include a fantastic, sexy, sensual redhead who had stirred his life into a tempest.

He could hear Duke threatening him, warning him to not hurt her and then admitting he had never talked to another man about that before. Why had Duke confronted him—even more seriously, threatened him? And Duke had known exactly what he was doing.

Wyatt shook his head. He couldn't answer his own questions and Duke remained a puzzle, but he had a feeling if

Destiny went back to Chicago missing him, he might be in a big heap of trouble when Duke returned to Verity if she came back for the show. That might be one more bit of trouble she had stirred into his life.

Wyatt hit the steering wheel with the palm of his hand. He missed her and wanted her. How long was it going to take to get over her? How long before she would be out of his thoughts?

He wanted her back in Verity. His life was going to be quiet and dull for the next few days. He didn't even know if he could get her television show out at the ranch.

"Destiny," he said, remembering driving with her beside him, her hand on his thigh, her flirting and teasing and sexy remarks.

Another plane went overhead and he gave it a dark look. She was flying away from him, back to her busy, fulfilling life, and she would forget Verity and its sheriff, their time together, everything here.

His spirits sank lower. He hadn't talked to her about seeing her again and that had been his fault. He pulled out his phone, looked at it and dropped it on the seat beside him. She was flying and wouldn't take the call.

"Dammit. Destiny." Why hadn't he made arrangements to fly up and see her?

Wyatt drove to the ranch, but unlike other times he didn't find the usual peace and quiet. He missed Destiny as much at the ranch as he had in Verity. He changed clothes, took a pickup and went to see if he could find some work to do and take his mind off Destiny.

By nightfall, he missed her beyond anything he had guessed possible. He hadn't felt this way since Katherine. The realization shocked him. Had he fallen in love without even knowing it?

He yanked out his phone to call Destiny. The moment he heard her voice, he felt better and worse at the same time. He wanted her in his arms, but he was glad to talk to her.

"Hi. I thought I'd see if you got in and if everything is okay."

"Yes. Thanks for the flight home. It was easy and a good flight. I'm just starting to unpack. I've been on the phone with my producer for the past hour. I think I have a show. Sorry, Wyatt, if you're still upset about Verity being on a television show."

"I've adjusted," he said. Then, as if the thought hit him from out of nowhere, he said, "I don't know where you live—a house, an apartment? Destiny, there's a lot I don't know about you."

She laughed. "We didn't spend a whole lot of time talking if you'll remember our moments together."

Oh, he did. Every hot one of them. "I miss you," he blurted, wondering about himself.

Her voice softened. "I miss you, Wyatt."

Silence stretched between them. "Let me know about the show."

"I will."

"Do you think I can get it at the ranch?"

"Wyatt, I don't have any idea what you can or cannot get on your television at your ranch," she said. "Are you okay?"

"I'm fine," he said, feeling anything but fine. "Do you see Duke, Amy and Virginia every day?"

"Heavens, no. Just Amy. I see a lot of Virginia, not so much of Duke."

"He's very protective of you."

"He is of all three of us when we travel with him. He's a great bodyguard, not that I've had any real trouble."

Wyatt settled back, listening to her talk, wanting her in his arms and finding talking to her was better than not talking to her, but he wanted her with him more than anything else.

When she finally said she had to go, it was two hours later. "Bye, Destiny. I miss you," he said again.

She broke the connection and he placed his phone on a table and sat back, lost in thought about her. He felt a huge empty void without her. How could he miss her this much? It would pass, he told himself again. Give it a week and he wouldn't feel this way at all.

He sat immobile, missing her, hurting, wishing he had made arrangements to see her, telling himself it was better to just break it off with her because he wasn't the marrying type. He was quiet and laid-back while Destiny was a whirlwind who wouldn't be happy settled on a ranch. He couldn't be in love. It was only lust, and she hadn't been in his life long enough for him to be all torn up over her going.

The next day he threw himself into work on the ranch, doing all the jobs that required physical labor, trying to keep his mind off Destiny, trying to keep busy and failing constantly. In the quiet of the ranch, or even with guys working around him some of the time, he couldn't stop thinking of Destiny.

By evening, he called her. When she didn't answer, his spirits sank lower. Was she out with someone else now? Even if she didn't have a serious or intimate relationship with anyone, he didn't want to think about her going out with someone else.

Monday he was back at the office in Verity. Everything in town reminded him of Destiny and being with her the past week. He was as miserable in Verity as he was on the ranch. She probably had moved on and was forgetting him by now, picking up the threads of her Chicago life and going on with living.

Thursday night he called her, as he'd done every night, and at the sound of her voice, he clutched the phone tightly. They just talked, more than they ever had. It was a two-hour phone call and before they hung up, she said she missed him and he told her he missed her, which seemed inadequate.

He ended the call and it hit him. He was in love with her. It was hopeless, something he had intended to avoid, but he loved her. He couldn't miss her this much, miss her constantly, and not be in love. She had filled his life in too many ways and now he wanted her back. Should he fly to Chicago and see her? She wouldn't want to come back to Texas.

He wondered if she really missed him as much. She said she did before ending their call, but how much did she mean it?

He knew how badly he missed her. He couldn't think at work and he had done some sloppy jobs at the ranch that he had had to do over.

He knew what he had to do.

He drove to Dallas and spent the next two days looking at wedding rings. Finally, wanting to impress her, he bought a ten-carat diamond ring with more diamonds and emeralds on the band. Now, if he could get a date to see her, he would fly to Chicago.

He was determined to see her and he was going to fly to Chicago. He had fallen in love with her without even knowing it, while trying to guard against doing any such thing.

When he was back home, he sat looking at the engagement ring he had bought and he felt ridiculous. He didn't know what she felt and he didn't want to tell her on the phone for the first time that he loved her.

He closed the box and put the ring in a bottom drawer while he sat staring into space, something he seemed to be doing a lot of since she had gone home. She had swept into his life, stolen his heart, left him in tangled knots and then left.

He picked up his phone to call and talk again.

Sunday night Destiny worked late. She had every night since she had returned from Texas. As she sat on her bed

and reviewed a script for the newest show, she couldn't
keep her mind on the words in front of her. It kept wander-
ing to Wyatt. She wondered whether he ever watched her
show or if he had even tried. He hadn't seemed to know
whether he could get it at the ranch, so she imagined he had
forgotten all about it. With each passing day, she missed
him more. He called her each night, so he must miss her
some, but he hadn't suggested that she come back to Texas
and he hadn't said he was coming to Chicago.

She punched the pillows behind her, then checked her
cell phone next to her on the blanket. She was waiting for
his nightly call. Wyatt kept his heart sealed away, avoiding love. Was he going to let life pass him by because he
didn't want to risk another hurt? Was she going to love him
to no avail, just because he wouldn't risk loving again?

When the phone rang, she yanked it up, glad to hear
from him yet almost angry with him. She wanted more
from him than these long nightly conversations that didn't
tell her anything about his feelings. She settled back to
talk, wondering where they were going and how long
things would go on this way, which was not typical of
Wyatt, who was a decisive person.

After two hours he told her goodbye and ended the call.
She sat staring at her phone. "Wyatt, why don't you come
see me? I love you, Wyatt," she whispered.

She looked into her open closet, her gaze resting on her
suitcase. Maybe if he wouldn't come to Chicago, she would
go to Texas. She stared at the suitcase, wondering about
Wyatt's feelings. Why hadn't he come to see her or asked
her to come back? Two-hour calls every night had to mean
something. But what? How deeply did his feelings run?

Of all men for her to fall in love with—it was one she
couldn't figure out.

Ten

Wyatt sat at his desk at the ranch trying to go over his bookkeeping, the figures he needed to give his accountant, but he couldn't concentrate. His cell phone beeped and he saw it was his foreman. "Brant?"

"Wyatt, there's a bright red limo that's turned up the road to the house. Want me to stop and see who it is and what they want?"

Startled, Wyatt stood and his heart started to pound. "No. I know who it is, I think. I'll go watch for them. Thanks." His heart raced. Jamming the phone into his pocket, he went outside on the east side of the house that gave a good view of the road. He saw a plume of dust in the distance and then a red speck that soon became a long red limo.

"What the hell?" he mumbled. He didn't take his eyes off the limo as it finally neared the house. As he started down the steps the limo swept past him along the drive to the front of the house.

"Dammit," Wyatt swore, striding back through the house to the front door. Through the windows he saw the red limo turn and head back toward the highway and he ran for the door to yank it open.

Wyatt stopped in his tracks. Destiny stood beside a suitcase and a carry-on. Her purse hanging on her shoulder, dressed in tight-fitting jeans and her favorite red sweater, she stood facing him as the red limo disappeared down the ranch road.

He realized he was standing there and staring at her. He dashed down the steps, taking them three at a time, and ran to her.

"What are you doing here?" he said, looking into her wide, green eyes. He didn't give her a chance to answer. He swept her into his arms and kissed her, holding her tightly against him, wondering if this was a dream and he would wake up.

Her arms wrapped around his neck as he picked her up, still kissing her, and he carried her into the house and kicked the door closed behind him. He headed to the nearest downstairs guest bedroom, stepping inside and shoving the door closed.

Over an hour later, he rolled over, taking her with him. He looked down at her. "Hi," he said.

"Hi, yourself," she answered, gazing up at him wide-eyed and solemn.

"This was a surprise."

"I suppose it is," she said, trailing her fingers over his chest.

"Want to tell me what's going on? What are you doing here?"

"We've had a lot of long phone calls, but nothing much else. I've missed you, Wyatt," she said, sounding uncertain and cautious.

His heart began to drum. "Darlin', I've missed you so much, it's been hell. Destiny, I shouldn't have let you go home like that, but I didn't know my own feelings. You made me fall in love with you. I wasn't going to do that, but I did. I did, I have. I love you," he declared.

"Wyatt! I love you. I don't know what happened to either one of us. You're a cowboy, a Texas rancher and you always will be. You're quiet and you want a quiet life. I'm none of that."

"Hardly," he said, grinning. "You wrecked any peace and quiet in my life. You're the center of attention everywhere you go. Neither of us is going to change either. Another Calhoun to take hold of a Milan and change him completely."

"I don't think there is a shred of a feud between this Calhoun and Milan," she said, kissing his throat and looking up at him mischievously.

"Wyatt, I've loved you almost since the first night we went out," she said and he let out his breath, drawing her to him and kissing her hard and long, wanting to let her know every way possible that he loved her.

Suddenly he stopped. "Stay right here. Don't go anywhere," he said as he got up and left.

"Where would I go like this?" Destiny asked an empty room. She scooted up, pulling a sheet beneath her arms and wondering where he had gone. His words echoed again and again—he loved her.

He came back to slip beneath the sheet with her. "Destiny Jones, will you marry me?" he asked.

Her heart pounded with joy as she threw her arms around him. "Yes, oh, yes."

He kissed her and in minutes he leaned away and fumbled in the bed to hand her a box. "I got this for you."

Her eyes widened. "Wyatt, I'm surprised. Since I went

back to Chicago, we haven't even been dating—" She
opened the box and gasped. "Oh, Wyatt, it's beautiful."
She threw her arms around him to kiss him again. "I love
you," she said after a long kiss.

"I love you, Destiny. I should have told you before you
went back to Chicago, but I didn't know my own feelings."

"I thought you didn't care. When did you decide that
you're in love?"

"I care. I love you with all my heart, but I didn't realize it until you were gone. Destiny, it's been hell without
you. Hon, we've got so many problems."

She laughed and looked at him, throwing her arms
around him again to kiss him. Finally, she leaned back.
"Now, tell me about all the problems we have…after you
put that ring on my finger."

She held out the ring and he took it to slip it on her
finger. "A perfect fit," she said. "It's the most beautiful
ring I've ever seen. Diamonds and emeralds. Perfect." She
looked up at him. "So what are the problems?"

"You won't want to live on the ranch. You have a television show in Chicago. I do want to live on the ranch. I
work in Verity."

She giggled. "We'll work it all out. You'll see. You have
your own airplane. We don't have to be together every minute. Shows don't last forever and I have other things in my
life I want to do. I might have a book career. There are jobs
in Dallas and—" She stopped, realizing she was babbling.
She took a breath and smiled at him. "Or I just might retire and have our babies. You do want babies, don't you?"

"Yes, as a matter of fact, I do now that you're going
to be their mother. Little girls just like you so we always
have excitement in our lives. I've spent the first half of my
life resting up for what's coming." His smile lit up those
amazing blue eyes.

"Wyatt, we can work through any problem as long as you love me and I love you and we're together a lot of the time."

He wrapped his arms tighter around her. "Well, so much for problems."

"Did you know I have a suitcase out in front of your house?"

"It won't go anywhere. I'll get it when I put on clothes, which isn't going to happen for a little while longer."

"Why not?"

"I'm going to make love to my fiancée."

How she loved the sound of that. She leaned in to kiss him before a thought struck her. "Wyatt, I need to tell Mimi and Desirée. Mimi is going to have to start liking Milans. She warned me you might be sneaky."

"I'll forgive her. And I want to tell all my family, too. I want you to meet my mom and dad."

"A judge. He may not approve of me."

"He's a man. He'll approve of you and if I love you, my mom will love you."

"Even when they find out I'm a Calhoun?"

"They managed with Madison. They will with me. Let's have this wedding soon."

"As soon as possible. Wyatt, I missed you so much. I didn't have any idea what you felt."

"From here on, you will always know. I'll tell you every morning and every night and all the times in between that I can. I love you, Destiny. I just didn't know it and didn't know how much."

She wiggled her fingers, looking at her ring. "Mrs. Wyatt Milan. That sounds beautiful." She wrapped her arms around him to kiss him. "A wonderful, joyous and exciting November wedding," she said, just before her mouth covered his.

* * * * *

REQUEST YOUR FREE BOOKS!

2 FREE NOVELS PLUS 2 FREE GIFTS!

HARLEQUIN®

Desire

ALWAYS POWERFUL, PASSIONATE AND PROVOCATIVE

YES! Please send me 2 FREE Harlequin Desire® novels and my 2 FREE gifts (gifts are worth about $10). After receiving them, if I don't wish to receive any more books, I can return the shipping statement marked "cancel." If I don't cancel, I will receive 6 brand-new novels every month and be billed just $4.55 per book in the U.S. or $4.99 per book in Canada. That's a savings of at least 13% off the cover price! It's quite a bargain! Shipping and handling is just 50¢ per book in the U.S. and 75¢ per book in Canada.* I understand that accepting the 2 free books and gifts places me under no obligation to buy anything. I can always return a shipment and cancel at any time. Even if I never buy another book, the two free books and gifts are mine to keep forever.

225/326 HDN F4ZC

Name _____ (PLEASE PRINT)

Address _____ Apt. #

City _____ State/Prov. _____ Zip/Postal Code

Signature (if under 18, a parent or guardian must sign)

Mail to the **Harlequin® Reader Service:**
IN U.S.A.: P.O. Box 1867, Buffalo, NY 14240-1867
IN CANADA: P.O. Box 609, Fort Erie, Ontario L2A 5X3

**Want to try two free books from another line?
Call 1-800-873-8635 or visit www.ReaderService.com.**

* Terms and prices subject to change without notice. Prices do not include applicable taxes. Sales tax applicable in N.Y. Canadian residents will be charged applicable taxes. Offer not valid in Quebec. This offer is limited to one order per household. Not valid for current subscribers to Harlequin Desire books. All orders subject to credit approval. Credit or debit balances in a customer's account(s) may be offset by any other outstanding balance owed by or to the customer. Please allow 4 to 6 weeks for delivery. Offer available while quantities last.

Your Privacy—The Harlequin® Reader Service is committed to protecting your privacy. Our Privacy Policy is available online at www.ReaderService.com or upon request from the Harlequin Reader Service.

We make a portion of our mailing list available to reputable third parties that offer products we believe may interest you. If you prefer that we not exchange your name with third parties, or if you wish to clarify or modify your communication preferences, please visit us at www.ReaderService.com/consumerchoice or write to us at Harlequin Reader Service Preference Service, P.O. Box 9062, Buffalo, NY 14269. Include your complete name and address.

HD13R

SPECIAL EXCERPT FROM

HARLEQUIN®

Desire

Read on for a sneak preview
of USA TODAY bestselling author
Janice Maynard's
STRANDED WITH THE RANCHER,
the debut novel in
TEXAS CATTLEMAN'S CLUB:
AFTER THE STORM.
Trapped in a storm cellar after the worst tornado to hit
Royal, Texas, in decades, two longtime enemies need
each other to survive…

Beth stood and went to the ladder, peering up at their prison door. "I don't hear anything at all," she said. "What if we have to spend the night here? I don't want to sleep on the concrete floor. And I'm hungry, dammit."

Drew heard the moment she cracked. Jumping to his feet, he took her in his arms and shushed her. He let her cry it out, surmising that the tears were healthy. This afternoon had been scary as hell, and to make things worse, they had no clue if help was on the way and no means of communication.

Beth felt good in his arms. Though he usually had the urge to argue with her, this was better. Her hair was silky, the natural curls alive and bouncing with vitality. Though he had felt the pull of sexual attraction between them before, he had never acted on it. Now, trapped in the dark with nothing to do, he wondered what would happen if he kissed her.

Wondering led to fantasizing, which led to action.

HDEXP0914

Tangling his fingers in the hair at her nape, he tugged back her head and looked at her, wishing he could see her expression. "Better now?" The crying was over except for the occasional hitching breath.

"Yes." He felt her nod.

"I want to kiss you, Beth. But you can say no."

She lifted her shoulders and let them fall. "You saved my life. I suppose a kiss is in order."

He frowned. "We saved *each other's* lives," he said firmly. "I'm not interested in kisses as legal tender."

"Oh, just do it," she said, the words sharp instead of romantic. "We've both thought about this over the last two years. Don't deny it."

He brushed the pad of his thumb over her lower lip. "I wasn't planning to."

When their lips touched, something spectacular happened. Time stood still. Not as it had in the frantic fury of the storm, but with a hushed anticipation.

Don't miss the first installment of the

**TEXAS CATTLEMAN'S CLUB:
AFTER THE STORM** *miniseries,*

STRANDED WITH THE RANCHER

by USA TODAY *bestselling author*

Janice Maynard.

*Available October 2014 wherever Harlequin® Desire
books and ebooks are sold.*

HARLEQUIN®

Desire

POWERFUL HEROES... SCANDALOUS SECRETS... BURNING DESIRES!

THE CHILD THEY DIDN'T EXPECT

by *USA TODAY* bestselling author

Yvonne Lindsay

Available October 2014

Surprise—it's a baby!

After their steamy vacation fling, Alison Carter knows
Ronin Marshall is a skilled lover and a billionaire businessman.
But a *father*...who hires her New Zealand baby-planning service?
This divorcée has already been deceived once;
Ronin's now the last man she wants to see.

But he must have Ali. Only she can rescue Ronin from the upheaval
of caring for his orphaned nephew...and give Ronin more of what
he shared with her during the best night of his life. But something is
holding her back. And Ronin will stop at nothing to find out what
secrets she's keeping!

_____

This exciting new story is part of the Harlequin® Desire's
popular *Billionaires & Babies* collection featuring
powerful men...wrapped around their babies' little fingers!

Available wherever books and ebooks are sold.

Talk to us online!
www.Facebook.com/HarlequinBooks
www.Pinterest.com/HarlequinBooks
www.Twitter.com/HarlequinBooks

HD73343

HARLEQUIN®

Desire

POWERFUL HEROES... SCANDALOUS SECRETS... BURNING DESIRES!

Come explore the *Secrets of Eden*—where keeping the past
buried isn't so easy when love is on the line!

HER SECRET HUSBAND
by **Andrea Laurence**

Available October 2014

Love, honor—and vow to keep the marriage a secret!

Years ago, Heath Langston eloped with Julianne Eden.
Their parents wouldn't have approved. So when the marriage
remained unconsummated, they went their separate ways without
telling anyone what they'd done.

Now family turmoil forces Heath and Julianne back into the same
town—into the same house. Heath has had enough of living a lie.
It's time for Julianne to give him the divorce she's avoided for so long—or
fulfill the promise in her smoldering glances and finally become his wife
in more than name only.

Other scandalous titles from Andrea Laurence's
Secrets of Eden:

UNDENIABLE DEMANDS
A BEAUTY UNCOVERED
HEIR TO SCANDAL

Available wherever books and ebooks are sold.

HD73345

HARLEQUIN®

Desire

TEMPTED BY A COWBOY
by Sarah M. Anderson

Available October 2014

**The 2nd novel of the *Beaumont Heirs* featuring
one Colorado family with limitless scandal!**

*How can she resist the cowboy's smile when it
promises so much pleasure?*

Phillip Beaumont likes his drinks strong and his women easy.
So why is he flirting with his new horse trainer, Jo Spears,
who challenges him at every turn? Phillip wants nothing but
the chase...until the look in Jo's haunted green eyes makes him
yearn for more....

Sure, Jo's boss is as jaded and stubborn as Sun, the
multimillion-dollar stallion she was hired to train. But it isn't
long before she starts spending days *and* nights with the sexy
cowboy. Maybe Sun isn't the only male on the Beaumont
ranch worth saving!

Be sure to read the 1st novel of the *Beaumont Heirs*
by Sarah M. Anderson
NOT THE BOSS'S BABY

Available wherever books and ebooks are sold.

www.Harlequin.com

HD73346